The Debit Acco

The Debit Account

by Oliver Onions

Copyright © 7/31/2015
Jefferson Publication

ISBN-13: 978-1515312512

Printed in the United States of America

All rights reserved. No part of this book may be reprinted or reproduced or utilized in any form or by any electronic, mechanical, or other means, now known or hereafter invented, including photocopying and recording, or in any form of storage or retrieval system, without prior permission in writing from the publisher.'

Contents

PART I THE COBDEN CORNER 4
   I 4
   II 7
   III 11
   IV 17
   V 21
PART II VERANDAH COTTAGE 25
   I 25
   II 30
   III 35
      FOOTNOTE: 44
   IV 44
   V 51
PART III WELL WALK 53
   I 53
   II 57
   III 64
   IV 71
   V 77
PART IV IDDESLEIGH GATE 85
   I 85
      FOOTNOTE: 91
   II 91
ENVOI SIR JULIUS PEPPER DICTATES 102
ENVOI 103

PART I THE COBDEN CORNER

THE DEBIT ACCOUNT

I

One day in the early June of the year 1900 I was taking a walk on Hampstead Heath and found myself in the neighbourhood of the Vale of Health. About that time my eyes were very much open for such things as house-agents' notice-boards and placards in windows that announced that houses or portions of houses were to let. I was going to be married, and wanted a place in which to live.

My salary was one hundred and fifty pounds a year. I figured on the wages-book of the Freight and Ballast Company as "Jeffries, J. H., Int. Ex. Con.," which meant that I was an intermediate clerk of the Confidential Exchange Department, and to this description of myself I affixed each week my signature across a penny stamp in formal receipt of my three pounds. I could have been paid in gold had I wished, but I had preferred a weekly cheque, and I took care never to cash this cheque at our own offices in Waterloo Place. I did not wish it to be known that I had no banking account. As a matter of fact, I now had one, though I should not have liked to disclose it to the Income Tax Commissioners. The reason for this reticence lay in the smallness, not in the largeness, of my balance. I had learned that in certain circumstances it pays you to appear better off than you are.

It was a Sunday, a Whit-Sunday, on which I took my walk, and on my way up from Camden Town across the Lower Heath I had passed among the canvas and tent-pegs and staked-out "pitches" that were the preparation for the Bank Holiday on the morrow. Tall *chevaux de frises* of swings were locked back with long bars; about the caravans picked out with red and green, the proprietors of cocoanut-shies and roundabouts smoked their pipes; and up the East Heath Road there rumbled from time to time, shaking the ground, a traction-engine with its string of waggons and gaudy tumbrils.

The Debit Account

I was alone. Both my *fiancée* and the aunt with whom she lived in a boarding-house in Woburn Place had gone down to Guildford to attend the funeral of a friend of the family—a Mrs Merridew; and as I had known the deceased lady by name only, my own attendance had not been considered necessary. So until lunch-time, when I had an engagement, I was taking my stroll, with a particular eye to the smaller of the houses I passed, and many conjectures about the rent of them.

You will remember, if you happen to know that north-western part of London, that away across the Heath, on the Highgate side, there stands up among the trees a lordly turreted place, the abode (I believe it then was) of some merchant prince or other. My eyes had wandered frequently to this great house, but I had lost it again as I had descended to the pond with the swans upon it, and approached the tea-garden that, with its swings and automatic machines, makes a sort of miniature standing Bank Holiday all the year round. During the whole of a youth and early manhood of extraordinary hardship (I was now nearing thirty-five) I had been consumed with a violent but ineffectual ambition, of which those distant turrets now reminded me.... I had been hideously poor, but, heaven be thanked, I had managed to get my head above water at last. Those horrible days were over, or nearly so. I had now, for example, a banking account; and though I seldom risked drawing a cheque for more than two pounds without first performing quite an intricate little sum, the data for which were furnished by my cheque, pass and paying-in books respectively, still—I had a banking account. I had also good boots, two fairish suits of clothes (though no evening clothes), an umbrella, a watch, and other possessions that, three or four years before, had seemed beyond dreams unattainable.

And when I say that I had for long been ragingly ambitious, I do not merely mean that I had constantly thought how fine it would be could I wake up one morning and find myself rich and powerful and respected. Had that been the whole of it, I don't think I should have differed greatly from the costers and showmen who dotted the Heath that Whit-Sunday morning. No; the point rather was, that I saw in the main how I was going to get what I wanted. I, or rather my coadjutor "Judy" Pepper and I between us, had ideas that we intended to "play" as one plays a hand at cards. Therefore, as I walked, I dare say I thought as much about that distant castellated house as I did about the far humbler abode I intended to take the moment I could find a suitable one.

I wandered among the alleys and windings of the Vale of Health, noting the villas with peeling plaster and the weather-boarded and half-dilapidated cottages that make the place peculiar; and I was ascending a steep hillock with willows at the foot of it and the level ridge of the Spaniards Road running like a railway embankment past the pines at the top, when, chancing to turn my head, I saw what appeared to be the very place for me.

It could not have been very long empty, for I had passed its door, an ivy-green one with lace curtains behind its upper panels of glass, without noticing the usual signs of uninhabitation. Then I remembered the approaching Quarter Day and smiled. The chances were that somebody had done a "moonlight flit" and had left the lace curtains up in order that his going might not be observed. There was no doubt, as I could see from where I stood, about the place being untenanted now, nor that it would not remain so for very long. I stood for a moment examining it from half-way up the hillock.

There was not much of it to examine. It was very small, fronted with stucco, and had a little square verandah built out on wooden posts over its tiny garden. More than that I could hardly see of it, but it adjoined a much larger house, and to this I turned my eyes. This larger house was a low, French-windowed dwelling, with a pleasantly eaved and flat-pitched roof, very refreshing to think of in these days of Garden City roofs and diminutive dormers; and its garden was well kept, and gay with virginia stock borders and delphinium and Canterbury bells in the beds behind. It seemed likely that formerly the two houses had been one.

I was descending the hillock for a closer view when I remembered that I could hardly expect to be shown round that day. I looked at my watch. It was half-past twelve, and my appointment, which was with Pepper, was not for another hour. There would be plenty of time for me to walk round by my turreted place and back by Hampstead Lane. I left the Vale of Health, crossed the Viaduct, and continued my saunter.

But I walked slowly, and in a deepening abstraction. The sight of that little house had set my thoughts running on my *fiancée* again. And as I presently took that little house, and married my *fiancée* not long afterwards, and as, moreover, my meditation of that morning has a good deal to do with my tale, I had better state at the beginning what the trouble was, and have done with it.

I had known Evie Soames for close on five years; and though I had loved her ever since the days when, with her skirt neither short nor long, and her hair neither loose nor yet properly revealing the shape of her slender and birch-like nape, she and I had attended the same Business College in Holborn, it had been only during the last six months that we had become engaged. On either of our parts a former engagement had ended abruptly; and this, for her sake at least, was the reason why I would gladly have had her anywhere but at Guildford that Sunday morning.

For it had been to the late Mrs Merridew's son that she had been engaged, and the affair had terminated with tragic suddenness indeed. You cannot but call it tragic when a young man is discovered, on his wedding morning, hanging by the neck from a hook in his bedroom door, with a letter in his pocket that only partly sets forth his reason for taking his life, leaving the rest for the medical evidence to determine—and then to be kept for very pity from his womenfolk. Yet this had happened four years before; and it was because I dreaded to revive the memory of it, and especially to revive the memories of those subsequent days when Evie must have tormented herself with vain and fruitless guessings at what a coroner and a jury-panel and a doctor in Store Street had smothered up among themselves, that I walked brooding and with downhung head.

And about women generally I had better confess myself at once as, past praying for, a Philistine. I subscribe to nothing whatever that this New Man so strangely risen in our midst nowadays appears to hold about the ancient and changeless feminine. And I take it that most men not profligates or fools will understand me when I say that I think there are some things that it is worse than useless that women should know, and that this sordid four-year-old business was one of them. To those born to knowledge, knowledge will come; the others will never know, no matter what the facts of their experience may be. Oh, I had seen these weak and vainglorious vessels go to Life's Niagara before, thinking to fill themselves at it—and had seen the flinders into which they had been dashed. Therefore I had deliberately resolved to stand between Evie Soames and many things. I ever thought of her as a flower, a flower of dewy flesh, joining its fragrance to that of the morning of her mind; and though I knew that that too lovely stage must quickly pass, perhaps into something better, I could never think of that passing unmoved. I was prepared to fight for a last—and perhaps impossible—protection of it. There was much knowledge that I would take on myself for the pair of us; a few more of life's weals and scars would make no difference to me.... And if you tell me that this was merely a foredoomed attempt to keep from her the knowledge of the world into which she had been born, very well: I accept the responsibility of that. At any rate, she might find what fantastic explanations she would of the mystery that I and the jury and a doctor in Store Street could have explained. I would open no door to admit her to horrors which would haunt her for ever though I closed it again in a flash.

I hope you see why I cursed that funeral, for bringing even the fringe of that old shadow back over us again.

The Debit Account

So absorbed was I in my meditation, that I passed my turreted house without noticing it. It was as I was approaching Waterlow Park that a clock striking one woke me out of my reverie. I shook off the weight of my thoughts. If this shadow had claimed Evie again, I must put something in its place when I met her and her aunt at Victoria that evening, that was all. I had now my coming interview with Pepper to think of.

I faced about and began to descend Hampstead Lane, suddenly occupied with business, to the exclusion even of Evie.

"Judy" (now Sir Julius) Pepper and I have been partners for ten years now; and while he is sometimes a little inclined to overrate what he calls my "imaginative qualities," I on the other hand have never been able sufficiently to admire his own hard, gay, polished efficiency. I still think of him, as I thought of him then, as of a diamond, that could encounter steel and come off with never an angle blunted nor a facet scratched; and if he in turn likens me to the handle in which that graver is set, and even to some extent to the guiding power, I pass that, thinking it as graceful to accept a compliment as to pay one. Exactly how our combination works is nobody else's concern; the important thing is, that between us we undoubtedly have made our mark since those days when he kept up appearances in Alfred Place, W., and I poked about the Vale of Health in search of a house that should come within the limits of my three pounds a week.

II

I was leaving the road at the Spaniards and striking across the West Heath when I came upon him. He also appeared to have been early, and to have been taking a walk to put away the time.

"Hallo!" I called, and he turned.

He was a short, rosy man of thirty-eight, with an inclination to plumpness that he only defeated by assiduous exercise; and his silk hat, "frocker" and grey cashmere trousers might have served some high tailor for an advertisement plate of perfect clothes. Perhaps they did, for I don't think that at that time he paid for them otherwise. His shirts and undergarments, of which he spoke with interest and readiness, were also perfect; and he not only made me feel in this respect like some rough bear of a Balzac, always in a dressing-gown, but even gave me, though quite without offensiveness, that and similar names. He gave me, in fact, this one now.

"Well, my dear Balzac!" he said, his rosy face breaking as suddenly into a smile as if a hundred invisible gravers had magically altered its whole clean modelling. "Out seeking an appetite?"

I laughed. "You're walking last night's supper off, I suppose?"

"N-o," he said, as if impartially looking back on whatever the excellent meal had been. "No—I'm scaling fairly low just now—just over the eleven stone. What are you, by the way?"

"Sixteen and a half—but then look at my size!"

He had the neatest and smallest and most resolute mouth, from which came speech so finished that I never heard a slurred word fall from it. He made it a little bud now, and whistled.

The Debit Account

"Sixteen and a——! I say, you'd better sign on at one of those shows I saw over there!"

"Well, with you as showman I dare say we should make it pay," I answered, falling in with this conception of our respective rôles.

His smile vanished as magically as it had come.

"Well, that's what we're going to talk about," he said; "but after lunch will do.... What sort of a tree do you call that, now?"

That was one of Judy's little affectations. He knew as well as I did that the tree at which he pointed was a birch, and I had thought, the first time I had exposed this dissimulation in him, that he would not try it on again. Fond hope! Though you knew that Pepper was laughing in his sleeve at you, and let him see you knew it, his face remained translucent and impenetrable as adamant.... So he took it as a piece of new and interesting information that the tree was a birch, and we walked on....

I had first met Pepper, or rather he had first spotted me, at the F.B.C., and we were both still at the offices in Waterloo Place. But while Pepper still moved his little wooden blocks (representing trains and ships) about vast box-enclosed maps with glass lids that shut down and locked, solving for the Company intricate problems of transport and the distribution of produce and manufactured stuff, he had already crossed the line that divides the Mercantile from the Political, or at least from the Administrative. Already that highly tempered cutting-point of manner had made a way for him into circles where I have never been at my ease; and dining once a month or oftener with the President and a Permanent Official of the Board of Trade, he was a valuable channel of information in such matters as Arbitration and the settlement of Trade Disputes. And he had been quicker than I to see the Achilles' heel of our complicated mercantile economy. Hitherto this vulnerable spot had been conceived to lie in Production, as in the last resort it certainly does; but short of that and actual industrial war, there was the equally effective and less perilous paralysis, the secret of which lay in Distribution. Shipping lines, railways and the postal organisation were the real nervous system; and Judy Pepper, strike-preventer rather than strike-breaker, was getting the ju-jitsu of it at his finger ends long before Syndicalism became aware of one of its most potent weapons.

You will see the manifold bearings of this on a Democratic Age.

And it was no less bold a move than our secession together from the F.B.C. and setting up on our own account that we were to discuss at lunch at the Bull and Bush that day.

We walked along a short street with cottages on one side and a high wall on the other, passed under the fairy-lamps of the Bull and Bush arch, and sought one of the little trellised bowers at the edge of the lawn.

Waiters always bestirred themselves to attend to Pepper, and the two who approached us at once neglected earlier comers to do so. Pepper gave his order, and we went through the Sunday "ordinary." Then he ordered coffee and liqueurs, bidding the waiter leave the bottle of *crème de menthe* on the table and not disturb us again. He lighted a cigar; I, not yet a practised smoker, fumbled with a cigarette, at the pasteboard packet of which I saw my ally's glance; and then, spreading a number of papers before him, he plunged into business.

It was highly technical, and I will not trouble you with more of it than bore on our immediate secession from the F.B.C.—a step to which I was strongly averse.

"You see," Pepper urged presently, "this Campbell Line award precipitates matters rather." (I shook my head, but he went on.) "As a precedent it's going to make an enormous difference. I'll show you the Trinity Master's statement presently.... No, no, wait till I've finished.... It means among other things a revision of the whole Campbell scale, and the other lines will have to follow. Then that'll make trouble with Labour, and Robson and the Board of Trade come in. Here's Robson's letter; better make a note of it. You don't write shorthand, do you?"

"N-o."

"Hm! You hardly seem quite sure whether you do or not!... Well, I'll get Miss Levey to make an abstract for you. Here's what he says...."

And he began to read from the letter.

As he did so I was wondering what on earth had made me tell him I didn't write shorthand. I do write shorthand. I keep, as a matter of fact, much of my private journal in shorthand, and I had not the slightest objection to Pepper or anybody else knowing of my accomplishment.... And yet, as if Pepper had somehow taken me off my guard, that doubtful "N-o" had come out. I bit my lip.

"Well," he concluded, folding the letter again, "there you have it. Of course I see what you mean about our using the F.B.C. for the present, merely as a going machine; but this seems to me to outweigh that.... You still don't think so?"

I still did not. Laboriously, for I never could make a speech in my life, I set my reasons before him. He nodded from time to time, opening and shutting his slender silver pencil.

"So you still think wait?" he mused by-and-by. It was evident that I had not spoken in vain.

"You can be going ahead with all you want to do as we are, and for the rest I'd wait and see what happened."

"Of course there's this war——" he admitted reluctantly.

"It's not the war. It's what'll happen after the war."

"Well," he said, with a shrug, "you know you're my heaven-sent find, and that I'm going to keep you to myself.... So we wait? That's decided?"

"Wait," I repeated doggedly.

Then, as if he had sufficiently tested my belief in myself, that smile broke over his agate of a face again. He leaned back to look at me.

"You're an extraordinary chap!" he positively sparkled fondness at me. "What are you getting now at the F.B.C.—three pounds?"

"Still I say wait," I said, nodding once or twice.

"And getting married on it!" he marvelled.

"Almost immediately."

Then Pepper laughed outright. "Well, I won't say you're like the chap who asked for a rise to get married on. 'You get married—you'll get the rise then!' his boss told him." Then, the smile going out again, he added, "And suppose we're forestalled on this new scale of rates?"

I spoke with strongly suppressed energy. "They can't forestall you and me. Don't you see? Don't you see we're *hors concours*—in a class by ourselves? We are what they can only make a bluff at being—ever! 'There is a tide'—but it hasn't got to be taken before the flood!"

He took the whole of me in in one shining look, as a camera might have seen me. He was openly admiring me.

"By Jove," he burst out, "but you don't lack confidence!... Of course you see the joke?"

The Debit Account

"You mean—'Jeffries, J. H., Int. Ex. Con., £3'—two-ten for his suits—eighteenpence for his dinners—getting married—and still hanging back from this because it's going to pay fifty times better twelve months from now?" That, I took it, was the joke.

"And you're quite—quite—sure?" he dared me for the last time, his face radiant.

I brought my hand softly down on the table. "Yes!" I cried. "I'm talking what I *know*—you're only talking what you *think*!"

His small manicured hand flew out to my great one.

"Oh—bravo!" he cried. "Wait it is, then. By Jove, when it does come, you'll have deserved it!... Here, shove your glass over—I believe you're entirely right—but if it was only for your consummate cheek we should have to drink to it!"

And he filled up the two glasses with the vivid green liqueur again, touching his against mine.

I left him shortly after, or rather he left me in order to keep one of his urgent and mysterious appointments; and I wandered slowly down towards my own abode.

This was a large upper room near the Cobden Statue—a proximity that for some reason or other always afforded my partner-to-be private mirth. I had taken it because its size fitted it both for living purposes and for the storing of the things I had got against my marriage as well. It was the fourth of the five floors of a new, terra-cotta-fronted, retail drapery establishment (experience had taught me that the biggest rooms are always over shops); and from its plate-glass windows below to its sham gables held up like pieces of stage scenery by iron braces above, it was a mass of ridiculous ornament—coats of arms, swags of fruit and flowers, and feeble grotesques with horns and tails and grins, the whole looking as if it had been squeezed on from some gigantic pink icing-tube such as they use for the modelling of wedding-cakes. But I lived inside it, not outside, and I had made the place exceedingly comfortable. I had no fewer than four large windows, two looking over the High Street, one diagonally from a rounded corner, and the fourth over the little railing-enclosed garden of a neighbouring crescent. As I was high enough up to dispense with blinds and curtains, these four windows admitted a flood of admirable light on an interior that, large as it was, was over-furnished; and there was no frippery to prevent my throwing up my sashes and looking down among the terra-cotta gargoyles on the walking hats below.

Evie and I had done much of our six months' courting in second-hand dealers' shops. Resolving that our engagement should be a short one, and knowing that those who have little either of money or time have, in furnishing as in everything else, to pay through the nose for their purchases, we had started at once. What had remained of a sum of money Evie's aunt had long had in trust for her against her one day setting up housekeeping on her own account had enabled us to do this. At first the sum had been one hundred and fifty pounds; a former purchase of clothing, of which only the black garments had ever been worn, had reduced it by more than a third; and of what had become of more than half the balance my light, lofty room now bore witness.

It improved my spirits to be among our joint belongings, and by the time I had made tea for myself, much of my despondency of earlier in the day had gone. I looked round, and began to tell myself over again the story of our acquisitions. There was not a piece that did not contribute its chapter. That bow-fronted chest of drawers with the old mirror on it we had first seen on a pavement in Upper Street, Islington; and we had had a long debate in Miss Angela Soames' sitting-room in Woburn Place before deciding to buy it—a debate much interrupted by less practical matters, with Miss Angela's pink-shaded lamp turned economically low, and Miss Angela herself intelligently off to bed. I had only to look at our odd assortment of chairs in order to see Evie again as she had stood in the dim back parts of this shop or that—to see again the whites of her eyes, brilliant as if her skin had been a Moor's, her hair dark as a black sweet-pea, the round neck with the little pulse in it, and the slender, just-grown lines of bosom or back or hips as she stooped or straightened. Over one extravagance her voice had broken out in shocked and delicious reproach; over another happy find she had had to turn away lest the dealer should see her eagerness and increase the price; and there had been laughs and bickerings and confusions and byplays without number.... I have become something of a connoisseur since then; but nothing I have acquired at Spink's or Christie's means to me what those coppery old Sheffield cream-jugs and caddies and those now-valuable sketches of Billy Izzard's meant....

Then, at seven o'clock, I washed, put on my hat, and went out. Evie and her aunt were due to arrive at Victoria at a quarter to eight.

I picked them out by their attire far down the platform, and advanced to meet them. With a leap of relief I noted Evie's little quickening as she saw me. Black "suited" Miss Angela Soames—suited her tower of white yet young-looking hair, as it also suited her habits of rather aimless retrospect and toying with stingless memories; but I hoped that Evie's present wearing of her four-year-old mourning would be her last. Naturally, she had not passed the day without tears. Her eyes were large, sombre patches; she held in her hand a little hard ball of damp handkerchief; and I noticed that a little graveside clay still adhered to the toes of her boots. But I judged that a night's rest would set her up again, and as we rumbled in a bus past the Houses of Parliament and up Whitehall, I bespoke her time for the afternoon of the morrow. I asked her, could she guess why? and, putting the screwed-up handkerchief away, she said something about the F.B.C.

"No," I replied,—"not directly, that is."

"Mr Pepper?"

"No."

Then, the decorum of her sorrow notwithstanding, she gave my sleeve a quick, light touch.

"*Not* a house, Jeff—you don't mean that you've found a *house*!"

But I refused to tell her. It was better that her mind should be occupied with guessing.

III

As I have said, I took that house in the Vale of Health. It wanted only three weeks of the June Quarter, so that I had to take it or leave it without overmuch delay. Evie and I went up to see it on the following day, and a scramble indeed we had to force our way through the Bank Holiday crowds. It took me nearly half-an-hour to get the key at the neighbouring tea-garden, where I had been told I must apply; on that day, they said, they couldn't be bothered; but I got it, and at the mere sight of the outside of the little house Evie gave a soft "Oh!" of pleasure.

"*What* a little darling!" she said. "Look—a separate tradesmen's entrance—and a little garden—and the Heath at our very door! I wonder what it's like inside!" she added, much as she still scans the handwriting and postmark of a letter for a minute for information she could have at once by opening it.

"I don't know yet," I replied.

"You dear, not to have seen it before me!"

I put the key into the glass-panelled door, and we entered.

Later I came to hate that little house; but that day, with Evie's spirits still a little tremulous, I did not dwell on drawbacks. It had only four rooms, two on each floor, and we walked straight from the street into the room that later became our dining-room. Behind this lay the kitchen, completing our ground-plan. Facing the door by which we had entered, and with a triangular cupboard underneath it, rose a carved and worn wooden staircase, that turned on itself after three or four steps and gave access to the floor above. Here the drawing-room exactly repeated the dining-room, as did the single bedroom the kitchen. But the drawing-room, besides having an extra window over the street door, had also the feature I had seen from the hillock on the previous day—the platform or verandah built out on wooden posts over the garden. This was gained by two steps and a glass door at the end of the room, and it provided me with my first disappointment. For, when I stepped out on to it, I found that we had *no* garden. The garden belonged to the adjoining house, the tenant of which had, moreover, secured his privacy by building in our little platform with a screen of boards and trellis. There would be just room enough on our little quarter-deck for a tea-table and a couple of chairs; but of prospect, save for the side of the hillock, had we none. For the rest, ceilings sagged, the worn old floor creaked and did not seem over-safe, the panelling (the whole place was wood-lined) was badly cracked, and the late tenants had turned the bath into a dustbin and general receptacle for rubbish.

I saw Evie warm to the drawing-room, our best room, at once. Already in her mind she was arranging our furniture. I, for my part, content to see her kindling interest, began to poke my nose into corners, making notes of such things as waterpipes, locks, window fastenings and the like. I squeezed into the narrow bathroom again; I am a little squeamish about baths, and, not much liking the pattern of this one, was wondering whether it could be altered; but the room was little more than a prolongation of a bedroom cupboard out over the staircase, and there would have been no changing the bath without pulling half the interior down. I bumped my head against its floor as I descended the stairs again, and passed into the diminutive yard that had the verandah for a roof. There I inspected a coal-house, and peeped through a knot-hole into my neighbour's garden. Then I sought Evie in the drawing-room again.

"Well?" I said, smiling, as she advanced to meet me....

Outside, the air was jocund with the incessant sounds of singing, calling, penny trumpets, the steam organs of the distant roundabouts, and all the bustle of the holiday. From our little verandah we could see the sides of the hillock dotted with picnic parties and coster lads in their bright neckerchiefs and girls in feathers and black lamb's-wool coats, making love after their own fashion. A party came round the house, singing and playing on mouth organs a dragging sentimental song—arms linked about necks, feet breaking into little step-dances, and feathers shaking from time to time to kisses that resembled assaults; and I was glad of it all. It was precisely what I would have chosen for Evie that day. She was dressed in brown again; a brown jacket, brown velvet skirt, close brown toque of pheasants' feathers, and brown shoes that showed their newness under their slender arches as she walked; no more black! For Life, after all, was made for joy. We had youth, she and I, in a truer sense than that of fewness of years—we had the youth which is Hope. Oh, I thought, let us then meet the years to come singingly—if a little stridently no matter—believing in our luck—full and spilling over—and taking as it came, like these outside, all the fun and dust and heat and perspiration of the fair! So I thought, and Evie too took the contagion. We were standing by the glass door of the verandah when suddenly she crushed herself hard and impulsively against me. I knew what she meant. It did not need the little tight grip of her hand to tell me that all was now "all right." I drank those tidings from the deep wells of her eyes. And because the flesh had little part in this promise, but must for once give place to other things, I did not seek her lips. Instead, my own moved for a moment about her hair....

Then a burst of catcalling caused us to fly from the verandah doorway. We had been seen from the hillside by the party with the mouth organs. Evie, adorably red, gave a low laugh ... and this time I did kiss her, to fresh cheers and calls of "Wot cher!" The lads and lasses outside did not see the caress, but perhaps, after all, it was not very wonderful thought-reading.

Then, after another delighted tour, we locked the house up and came out on to the Heath again.

And now that the scales of preoccupation were removed from our eyes, we could look on all the life and colour and movement spread before us and feel ourselves part of it. It was well worth looking at. There is a long ravine near the Viaduct; we looked across it through a bright stipple of sunny birches; and to close the eyes for a second or two only was to see, on reopening them, a new picture. Purple and lavender and the black lamb's-wool coats pervaded that picture; the colours were sown over the hillside like confetti. They moved slowly, as coloured granules might have moved in some half-fluid suspension; and spaces that one moment were spangled with them, the next were unexpectedly empty patches of green. I am speaking of the thing in the mass, as of a panorama. Doubtless the sprinkling of white that lay everywhere would resolve itself on the morrow into torn paper, to be laboriously impaled on spiked sticks and carried away in baskets; doubtless to-day much of it on a nearer view would consist of impure complexions and rank odour; but it was strong and piping-hot Life, inspiring, infinitely analysable, and irresistibly setting private griefs and joys and over-emphasised sensations into place and proportion.... And as we left the Viaduct road and approached a great show in a hollow, the increasing din of a steam organ became as if we waded deeper and deeper into a sea, not of water, but of sound.

I only remembered that I still had the key of the little house in my pocket as we pushed and jostled through the crowded town of striped canvas that covered the Lower Heath. My fingers encountered it as we took a back way behind a long fluttering sheet against which cocoanut balls smacked every moment. It was necessary to return with it; and, as men behind the lace-curtained caravans began to make ready the naphtha lights for the evening, we turned into another thoroughfare down which the purple and lamb's-wool and lavender and bright neckerchiefs poured as if down a river-bed. In twenty minutes we had reached the tea-garden again; I spied a couple in the act of leaving a leafy arbour that held a table awash with spilt beer; and I put Evie into a still warm seat and bade her hold it against all comers. I left her, and presently returned with two glasses, of which I had managed to retain the greater part of the contents; and I sat down by her.

"Did you give them the key?" she asked, seizing my arm.

"Yes, I gave them 'the' key. I'm going to see the agent to-morrow."

"Oh, Jeff!" She said it as if there was something miraculous in it that an agent might actually consent to be seen about that little house on the morrow.

"That is, unless to-morrow's a holiday too."

"Oh, you *must* go!" she broke out. "It would be *too* awful if we were to miss it!"

Then, as a waiter came with a sopping cloth to wipe down the table, we ceased to talk.

Already they were beginning to light up everywhere. The crowded garden became a complexity of ceaselessly moving shadows with a hundred little accidents of light—the flames of sudden matches, yellow shafts as people moved aside from windows, the twinkling festoons of the arbours, the gleam of liquid spilt on tables. A glow like that of a furnace rose behind the trees in front of us, and over the tree-tops rose swinging boats, sometimes one, sometimes two or three at a time, with lads standing with bent knees on the seats and the girls' feathers tossing and boas flying in the golden haze. The noise became a ceaseless twanging everywhere, and I watched with amusement a half-drunk but wholly happy sailor at the next table, who nodded sleepily from time to time, then looked with wideawake and amiable defiance about him, and had quite forgotten that he wore his companion's hat hearsed with black feathers.

"Do you want to change hats?" I said to Evie, with a glance at her pheasants' feather toque.

"No—but——" I saw her own glance at the sailor's thick wrist, which had appeared on our side of his companion.

The next moment, though with protests, she was leaning farther back in the shadow.

Then, close and in murmurs, we began to talk.

I am not going to claim for Evie that she ever had any very remarkable gift of tongues. I don't mean that on occasion she couldn't talk for half a day on end; but I do mean that beyond a certain point she displayed a diffidence, talk became something of an adventure to her, and she had a way of advancing upon a silence as if it was a fortified place, to be carried by assault, and not to be won by beleaguering. Therefore, seeing her now sensible of a new liberation and joy, I was not unprepared for little excesses, things said out of mere fulness, and perhaps even to be slightly regretted on the morrow.

Yet I didn't want fulness on the subjects of which she now began to ease her breast. I didn't want to hear of the events of the day before, nor of the people who had been there, nor of whether these people had or had not "thought it odd" that she should have become re-engaged. I didn't want to hear about the late Mrs Merridew's lingering and comatose illness. And when, in a burst of almost passionate candour, she spoke of the relief it was to be able at last to unburden herself thus, I would gladly have stopped her had I known how. But I lacked the courage to tell her, when she asked me whether I did not think it a good idea that she should keep nothing secret from me, that I thought it the worst of ideas.

"You see, Jeff," she murmured, out of a beautiful sense of rest and surrender, "I do so want ours to be a friendship as well as a marriage!"

Already the nearness and warmth of her had set me trembling. I don't know that I wanted more "friendship" than needs be; I wanted something, oh, far deeper and rarer. I wanted that full treasury of her warm blood and odorous hair and large and mobile eyes. Friendship? I laughed softly, and gathered these beauties closer.... Understand, I don't for a moment mean that she was unaware of these possessions of hers; I call that oval mirror that later we set up in our bedroom to witness that; but she merely wanted something else, being human, and wanted it the more, being feminine. And as she told me now what she wanted our marriage to be, she put me away a little, with her hands on my breast.

"Don't you, too, darling?" she appealed, with a look that put "friendship" quite out of existence....

"Don't I what, rogue?"

"Want it to be like that."

"No," I bantered, adoring her....

"Oh! Then there's something you won't tell *me*!... Very well," she pouted, "keep your old secrets, but I shall tell you everything for all that, just to shame you...."

With a laugh I was drawing her towards me again, when I was arrested by a circumstance so oddly trivial that I really hesitate to set it down. The first I knew of it was that with an involuntary and nervous start I had checked the movement, and had put her slowly away again, looking into her face as a moment before she had looked into

The Debit Account

mine. To explain what I saw there I must mention that, a few minutes before, the sailor and his girl had risen from the next table and lurched away, their heads together making an apex that wobbled over its base of purple skirt and wide trousers; but I had been only dimly conscious of the noise with which a fresh party had pounced upon their empty places. Now suddenly our alcove was filled with a raw crimson shine. Evie's face, as I held it away, was as if a stage fire glared upon it. And scarcely had the bloodshot light died away when it came again, another violent flood....

I had looked round in less time than it has taken me to explain this. It was only one of the newcomers playing with a penny box of Bengal matches. He struck another. This was a green one, and as he waved the spluttering thing about the shadows of leaves ran to and fro in our little interior.

Then as the match went out, all became an ashy darkness again.

Why, at the mere striking of those fusees, had all the life and joy suddenly gone out of me? I did not know.... But stay; I am not sure that in this I do not lie. Perhaps it would be nearer the truth to say that I would not know, and yet again that is not all.... Perhaps I had better pass on; you may know soon enough, if you care, what was the matter. Red and gold would now have been better suited to those two mainsprings of my life, my Love and my Ambition; but suddenly to change the gold into green, the hated hue of my past Jealousy....

Let me pass on. The thing will soon be clear.

For a minute and more I had hardly heard Evie's chatter, but presently I became conscious that she was repeating a phrase, as if a little surprised that she got no answer. I roused myself.

"Eh?... What were you saying, dear?" I apologised.

As if the striking of those matches had made an alteration in her too, her playfulness had vanished. Apparently another little access of candour had taken its place. Evidently I had missed some necessary link, for she was now murmuring, "Poor dear—I haven't been able to get her out of my head—it seems wrong somehow that I should be so happy and she——"

"She?... Who?" I asked in surprise, now fully awake again.

Evie mentioned a name. At the next table another crimson match went off, leaving, as it died down fumily, the yellow twinklings of the garden a bilious green. I spoke slowly. The name she had mentioned had been that of my own former *fiancée*.

"Kitty Windus?" I said. "What about her?"

Evie made no answer, but only stroked her cheek against the cloth of my shoulder—a familiar gesture of hers.

"I'm afraid I don't quite understand," I said.

Nor did I quite. I could not believe she was jealous. If Evie was jealous, never, never woman had had less cause. Except as the bitterest of mockeries, I had never been engaged to any woman but herself, for only that old horrible poverty and despair of mine had been the cause of my playing a trick with more of the falsely theatrical about it than of real life—the deliberate engaging of myself to one woman as a means to getting another. The impossible situation had lasted for a few months only, and had then ended in the abrupt vanishing, without explanation, of Kitty Windus from that part of London in which she had lived. From that day to this I had not set eyes on her.

I leaned over Evie. "Dearest," I said gently, "do you mean that there's something you would like to know about Kitty?"

Then, with a little shock, she seemed to realise that I might think what in fact had for the moment crossed my mind—that she was jealous of Kitty.

"Oh, Jeff ... no, no—really no!" she assured me in tones of which there was no mistaking the sincerity. "I didn't mean that—poor thing!—I was only joking when I said there was something you wouldn't tell me! Oh, do see what I mean, dear! It's only because *I'm* so happy that I want everybody else to be—Kitty too—everybody! Really that's all, Jeff!"

It was not quite all, though it was enough to make my heart a little lighter. Mingled with it was something very human that only endeared her to me the more. Her glow and vitality had always put poor Kitty's skimpiness completely into the shade, and what ailed her now was that wistful longing of the victress to be magnanimous that is the uneasy aftercrop of triumph. On herself it had all the effect of a generosity, but that, and not jealousy, was really it....

"Well, after all, we don't know that she isn't happy," I said cheerfully. "Anyway, she pleased herself, and—it's four years ago.... Just listen to the row!"

I was glad of the diversion that came just then. Led by a Jew's harp, the party at the next table had broken into "Soldiers of the Queen," and for the five hundredth time that day the song had "caught on" instantly. The whole garden was now vociferating it, standing on seats, dancing between the tables, their rising and falling heads a dark and bizarre tumult in the conflicting lights. At the gate of the garden a barrel-organ stopped and took up the same song in another key, but they drowned it:—

"Who've b—ee—een—my lads!

And s—ee—een—my lads!"

Talk in that uproar was impossible, and again there enwrapped us that strong sense of rich and rough and abundant life. As we leaned over our little table to watch, Evie's finger was moving in time to the song, and even the thought of the little house a few hundred yards away disappeared for a moment from my own mind. A chair with a couple of girls upon it broke, and there were shrieks and applause and whistles and laughter; and then the song began to die away. Cheers followed it, and cheers again, for throats cheered readily then; and then our neighbours of the next table formed themselves into single file, and, with a last shrill

"Who've b—ee—een—my lads!

And s—ee—een—my lads!"

marched round the garden and out into the crowds beyond. I seized my opportunity. Evie and I followed them, I with her tucked safely away under my arm; and we joined the dense stream that was already pouring southwards. And as I struggled for places on a bus at Hampstead Heath Station, my heart was grateful for that illusion of the day that had banished, first, the remnant of Evie's sorrow, and had afterwards cut short that impossible course of unmeasured confidences to which that moodiness had given rise.

IV

I began to foresee those inconveniences that afterwards made me hate that house in the Vale of Health as soon as I had signed my contract and got the key. The contract was for a year only, and as for any period less than three years the agents had refused to "do up" the place for me, I became plasterer, painter and plumber myself. I suppose that from the strictly conventional point of view Evie ought to have had no hand in this; indeed, she read me, from the "Etiquette" column of one of her weekly papers, a passage that informed me that between her choice of a house and her going into it as its mistress in the eyes of all the world a bride-elect ought to betray no knowledge of that house's existence; but as she delivered this from over the bib of an enormous apron, holding the journal in one hand, while the fingers of the other rubbed the lumps out of a bucket of whitewash, the knowledge came too late to be of much use. Anyway, there we were, with Miss Angela or an old charwoman or else nobody at all for chaperon, scraping walls, mixing paint, putting cracks, fixing shelves, dragging at obstinate old nails; and seeing that from the point of view of Etiquette we were already numbered with the lost, we made no bones about walking into a shop in Tottenham Court Road together and brazenly asking to be shown the bedstead department. After that we took tea, with never a human eye upon us, in my lofty room near the Cobden Statue. Doubtless this cut us off finally from that dim eschatological hope when even the devil shall have his respite of a thousand years. Our only solace was that we found ourselves in the company of a good many others who have to square their Etiquette with their opportunities as best they can.

But about those inconveniences. Why, with the whole Heath before them, the children on their way to or from school should make our doorstep their playground I didn't know; but they did, and it needed no gift of prophecy to see that when the schools closed later in the summer they would be an almost hourly nuisance. That was the first thing that struck me. Next, the crown of my head was like to be sore from many bumpings before I had learned to avoid the bathroom floor as I mounted our creaking, turning stairs. Next, ready as I should have been to secure my own garden from overlooking had I had one, I resented that screen of trellis that limited the view from our little balcony to the slope of hillside opposite. Add to these that not a window-sash fitted within half or three-quarters of an inch, that not a door was truly hung, that, wherever I wanted to make good a hinge or fastening, the woodwork was soft as a mushroom with old screwholes, and that I should have ruined a whole shopful of tools had I even attempted to level our splintery old floor, and you will see why I rejoiced to think that our tenancy might not be a very long one. But I need hardly add that, after all, these things weighed but a trifle against my impatience, and that I was careful not to let Evie suppose that I did not think our little nook the most delightful spot imaginable.

As a matter of fact I was compelled to leave a large part of the work to Evie; and capitally she did it. She had forgotten her old smattering of business training so completely that she always found it easier to go through her day's duties than she did to balance her expenditure afterwards in the highly ornamental "Housekeeper's Book" I bought for her; and while I was allowed my way in such unimportant things as where we should put our old-fashioned chests of drawers and Sheffield caddies and those sketches of Billy Izzard's, the department that began with the frying-pan and ended with general cleaning was hers. I had given her a second key, not only of the new house, but also of my own quarters in Camden Town; and sometimes at the F.B.C. I would look up from my work, gaze past the Duke of York's Column with its circling pigeons and away over the Mall, and wonder what she was doing now—taking our new dinner-service from its crates and washing it, peeping down the long cylinder of kitchen linoleum and wishing I was there to cut it to the floor, lighting fires to get rid of the damp, or (strictly against orders) scrubbing out the bath which, later, strive as I would, I could never successfully re-enamel. Then in the evening I would hasten for the Hampstead bus, stride up from the Heath Station, and, arrived at home, throw off my coat, put up shelves, fit carpets, see how my new paint (an ivory white) was drying, and only knock off when, not Etiquette, but the lateness of the hour and the distance I had to take Evie home compelled me.

I liked the daily life at the F.B.C. Our various departments were to a great extent isolated, so that the intermediate clerks like myself could only guess at the relation of their own portion of the work to the whole intricate business; but I have told you how I myself was privately "let in on the ground floor" by Pepper. I had three "Juns. Ex. Con." as my immediate subordinates, and they were first-rate fellows, and amusing company into the bargain. All three, Whitlock, Stonor and Peddie, were younger than I by some years; and as they were all bachelors, and there was plenty of time yet for them to begin to take their work very seriously, they showed not a trace of envy of me. Indeed, being rather "doggish" in their dress, and reckoning the work of the day as little more than a killing of time until the pleasures of the evening should begin, they even made something of a pet of their "Balzac in a dressing-gown"; and as if the nearness of our offices to Piccadilly put on them some responsibility that the character for gaiety of that gay part of London should not suffer through their negligence, they had an air of owning the quarter. They furnished drinks at Epitaux's as a man might in his own house, and introduced their companions at Stone's as if they had been veritable guests. True, funds did not often run to the old Continental over the way; but they knew by sight many of the loungers who entered its portals from four o'clock in the afternoon on, and would exchange intelligent glances over their filing or posting as suède boots, or picture hat, or something that looked as if it had stepped out of Stagg & Mantle's window tripped seductively by.

Pepper, of course, was my own immediate superior, as I was of my three boys; and while our private arrangement put me after office hours straightway on a level with the mandarins of the concern, we strictly kept our respective positions at Waterloo Place. I prepared drafts for him of such matters as Paying Ballast, Railway Digests, the daily postings at Lloyd's and the fluctuations of Insurance Rates; and these he changed into factors of policy in high council with the lords of other departments. His private office was immediately above ours; and twenty times a day his secretary, Miss Levey, descended the broad mosaic staircase or came down in the gilt and upholstered lift, either commanding my attendance, or bringing me instructions. It was a "wheeze" among my three boys to pose as her admirers, but I never thought she was quite so unconscious of their real thoughts as they supposed.

I was going to pass on; but while I am about it I may as well say a little more about this Miss Levey, and my reasons for regarding her as a person to be rather carefully watched. She was short, and a victim to her race's tendency to early stoutness; and as she had no neck, and always wore hats far too large for her, her appearance was top-heavy. Of her too large and prominent features her pot-hook nose was the most prominent. Her manner towards myself was that of one who would have liked to be familiar, but lacked the confidence; and doubtless her perpetual hovering on the confines of a liberty arose out of some slight acquaintance she had had with Evie in the days of her business training. As if Evie's health was as liable to fluctuations as the Export charts and Trade returns on our walls, Miss Levey never omitted to inquire after it each morning, becoming daily more *empressée* as our engagement proceeded; but so far she had not succeeded in what I divined to be her object, an invitation to renew the old acquaintance. And though I could keep the greater part of our intercourse strictly to business, I could hardly avoid occasional meetings on the stairs, in the lift, or sometimes a walk up Lower Regent Street with her as far as the Circus.

It was during the course of one of these short walks, one lunch-time, that, having obtained from me her daily bulletin, Miss Levey rather put me in a hole by asking me what I thought Evie would like for a wedding present. Secretly I neither wanted a wedding present from Miss Levey nor wished Evie to receive one, but I could hardly give her the slap on the face of telling her so. Instead I answered, a little abruptly, that I really didn't know—that it was awfully kind of her—and that she wasn't to think of it; but she did not take the hint. So, knowing her capacity for swallowing, but not forgetting snubs, and really feeling that perhaps I had gone a little too far, I hastened to repair a possible rudeness. We were approaching the tea-shop near the Circus at which I usually lunched; we reached it, and paused together on the kerb; and then, on the spur of the moment, I suggested that she should lunch with me. With a little demonstration of pleasure she accepted, and we entered and took our places at a small round table in the shadow of the pay-desk.

I knew, of course, that I had been cornered, and that she knew it too; but in these cases the thick-skinned person always has the advantage. I resolved that that advantage should be as slight as possible. And for a time—though probably not for one moment longer than she wished—I succeeded. As she ate her rissole and sipped her chocolate she talked with animation of this and that—the morning's business, the people in the crowded shop, the theatres, and so on; and then she returned to the subject of the wedding present, the date of my marriage, where we were going to live, and the rest of it. I was as reserved as my unwillingly given invitation allowed me to be, but presently I had to promise to ask Evie what form she would like the present to take. With that, Miss Levey went off at score, speaking of Evie as she had known her.

"I suppose she's prettier than ever?" she said. "Such a lovely girl I used to think her! I'm sure you're very lucky, Mr Jeffries, if you don't mind my saying so!"

I did rather mind her saying anything about it at all, but I answered quite conventionally that I considered myself very lucky indeed.

"Those were jolly days!" she passed on into reminiscence. "I loved that poky little old place in Holborn!... Do you remember the Secretary Bird, Mr Jeffries?"

I did remember Weston, the wan, middle-aged "professor."

"Poor old soul! I wonder if he's going with them to the new place? Of course you know they're pulling the old one down?"

"Yes."

"Such a huge one, that one in Kingsway! All the latest improvements—everything! But it won't ever be the same to me.... 'Not room to turn round'?... No, I suppose there wasn't, but I suppose I'm rather faithful to old places and old faces. You aren't, Mr Jeffries?"

"Not just because they're old," I fancied.

"Oh, I think I am, just because they're old!" she replied brightly.

From faces and places she passed to names, though—this was quite marked—only to certain ones; and I became rather obstinately silent except when she actually paused for a remark. For far more significant were the names she omitted than those she pronounced. These, indeed, she positively had the effect of shouting at me, and I suppose it was some heavy-handed delicacy that led her to speak of Weston but not of Archie Merridew, of Evie, but not of Kitty Windus and others she had known far better. I supposed her to be merely gratifying her racial greed for general (including personal) information, on the chance, so to speak, of turning up in the dustheap something she might later sell for twopence; and, noting one of her marked omissions, it occurred to me to wonder whether she might not have seen Kitty Windus, and, failing to get anything out of her, was now pumping myself and looking for an opening to pump Evie also. My eyes rested from time to time on her prominent-featured face and wide, high shoulders; and she did not know that I was wondering whether she was so deeply in Pepper's secrets that we should not be able to dispense with her services when he and I cleared out of the F.B.C. together.

I maintained my silence while she went on with her *Hamlet* without the Prince, that is to say, while she talked of the now demolished Business College without mentioning Archie Merridew, Kitty Windus, Louie Causton and the rest; and then, pleading an engagement, I rose. She rose too. With her purse in her hand, she made quite an ado about refusing to allow me to pay for the lunch to which I had invited her. "Please—or I shall feel as if we can't lunch together again!" she said; "let me see; sevenpence, that's right, isn't it? There! You will remember me to Evie, won't you?"

And she scrupulously put the sevenpence into one of my hands while with the other I held the door open for her to pass out.

I did not give Evie Miss Levey's message that evening, for when, at a little after seven, I reached the Vale of Health, I found Miss Angela there. The elder Miss Soames, I ought to say, regarded our wedding as so exclusively Evie's (myself sometimes appearing to have no part whatever in it) that I was constantly invited to share her own detached delight. Giving up Evie's bedroom only, she intended to stay on at Woburn Place; but from the number of offerings she brought us her own sitting-room was like to be sadly denuded. She brought, and if possible hid in a corner for us to discover after she had left, heavy old silver tablespoons, her shield-shaped embroidered fire-screen, her Colport dressing-table set with the little coral-like trees for rings, and other gifts; and it was in vain that Evie laughingly protested.

"But if you go on like this we shall have to have you come and live with us!" she said. "Make you up a bed on the verandah—but perhaps that's what she's really after, Jeff——"

But Miss Angela shook her head demurely, ignoring the joke. "No, no—young people ought to be alone; they don't want old things like me interfering. I shall be just as happy thinking of you both as if it was my own wedding."

And I really believe she was.

For the Etiquette of our preparations, Aunt Angela threw herself pathetically on my mercy.

Her sitting-room in Woburn Place, however, was not the only one that was rapidly becoming denuded. My own place with the terra-cotta festoons and hobgoblins was now more than half empty. But I was not relinquishing it yet. I knew I was committing a sentimental extravagance in thus being lord of two domiciles, but (Etiquette having to be considered) I did not wish to go into the new place until I should go there with Evie. So already two cartloads of my belongings had been fetched away, and that very day Miss Angela had been assisting in a task that more than any other seemed the beginning of the end—the removal of my carpet. They did not tell me of this removal. They allowed me to discover it for myself when I went, without light, upstairs into the drawing-room. They had already laid it down; my foot struck its softness in the dark; and I experienced a sudden little thrill of pleasure. It seemed to bring all so suddenly near....

They had crept up after me with a lamp to enjoy my surprise. The room really looked delightful, and all my sense of drawbacks vanished. Four glass candle-sconces with musical little drops—I had picked them up cheap in the street that runs from the Britannia to Regent's Park—were fastened to the walls, two between the window-bays over my breast-high mahogany bookshelves, the other two at the sides of the fireplace in the opposite wall; and across the windows themselves the long chintz curtains were drawn. Evie set the lamp down on the little table that folded almost to nothing against the wall, and tripped round with a taper, lighting up. All my chairs were there, and the couch for which I had ransacked half the catacombs of the Tottenham Court Road, and I can't tell you how pretty it all was, with its ivory woodwork, its dark blue and crimson blotted carpet, and the candle flames turning the polished glass lustres to soft sprinklings of gems. Miss Angela, delicate Pandar, seeing Evie's hand steal towards mine, affected to be very busy at the mantelpiece....

"So," I grumbled presently, "this is your idea of the cheapest way of lighting a room—candles at goodness knows how much a pound?"

"Well, there's no electric light," retorted Evie.

"And what have you left me at the other place? A bed and a broken chair, I suppose, to make shift with for three weeks and more!"

"*And* a jampot for your shaving-water. Quite enough for a bachelor."

"And I'm to get my meals out, I suppose, and pay twice as much for them."

But they only begged me to look where they had put Billy Izzard's two sketches—one on either side of the verandah door.

I had, in truth, begun to feel the least bit alarmed at the rate at which the money was going. Kitchens, I learned, cost like the dickens; but, as Evie frugally extinguished the candles again and led me down into her special province, I could not deny that that looked pretty too, with its bright tins, hanging jugs, overlapping rows of plates and saucers and the new linoleum of its floor. The dining-room, into which (as Evie said) "all the dirt was brought," had been left until the last, and was knee-deep in straw, torn packing-paper, split box-lids and cut string, and of course I grumbled again that good brown paper had been torn and useful string spoiled, until I was brought into good temper again by being allowed another peep at the lighted drawing-room—this time without Aunt Angela.

V

We were to be married at half-past ten on the following Saturday morning but one, at St. George's, Hart Street, Bloomsbury. We had chosen a Saturday because of our honeymoon, which was to be a steamboat trip either down the river to Greenwich or up the river to Hampton Court—we had not decided which. A good friend of mine, Sydney Pettinger, who had given me my start with F.B.C., had promised to give Evie away. Pepper would have done so, but Pepper always dazzled Evie a little. He was almost inhumanly never at a loss for a word.

Our little house was now quite ready. They had left me not so much as a chair in my room near the Cobden Statue. My pallet bed and my shaving-tackle were about all that remained within its walls, and I was on the point of disposing of the bed as it stood to a dealer in Queen's Crescent, when Billy Izzard proposed to me that he should take over the place.

Let me describe Billy Izzard as he was then—as he still to a great extent is for the matter of that, for his innumerable quarrels with dealers and intransigence on hanging committees have resulted in his being less well known than the high quality of his painting warrants. He was a tall, double-jointed, monkey-up-a-stick of a lad of twenty-four, with well-shaped features that always seemed a little larger than the ordinary (as if you saw them through a very weak lens), and two or three distinct voices, the most startling of which was the sudden, imperious tone into which he broke when he "saw" something—saw it absolute, in the flat, and as if it had never been seen before—but possibly you know his painting. He had exquisite manners, which he never used; he dressed in tweeds that made my own shaggy garments look like the finest broadcloth—they always seemed stuck over with fishing-flies; and, a sufficiently large studio being beyond his means until he should cease to quarrel with his bread and butter, he too had discovered the advantages of the large rooms that are to be found over shops.

He came up with his wedding present, yet another painting, just as I was contemplating the sale of my bed. The picture, wrapped in newspaper, was under his arm. He scratched his head under his porringer of a "sports" cap, looked round the big four-windowed room, and said, "Good light—south and east though—what?"

"South and east," I replied; and added, knowing Billy, "Rent paid monthly, in advance."

"How much?" he demanded.

"Twelve bob a week."

"Hm! Rather a lot for me," said the man whose practice (for his theory never amounted to much) has since been made the foundation of a whole school of modern painting. "Wish I hadn't brought you this now—I was offered three pounds for it—that would have paid for the first month——"

I hastened to grab the painting, to make sure of getting it. It was only a small flower group, a straggle of violets, a few white ones among them, in a lustre bowl, but the other day I refused sixty pounds for it.

"Too late, Billy," I said; "you know you can't fight me for it.... I'll throw you in my bed if you want the place, but you're not to give my name as a reference for your solvency."

"I think it might do," he said. "I could shut off some of the light, and I don't suppose they'd mind my making it an un-Drapery Establishment sometimes."

Billy was just beginning to paint flesh as truly and seeingly as he painted flowers.

With the exception of Aunt Angela's constant trickle, Billy's was our first wedding-present; but others followed quickly. Pepper, of course, contrived to get his joke out of his own very handsome offering. One day, at the end of one of our morning interviews in his office, he said: "Oh, by the way—I sent a small parcel off to you yesterday. I suppose 'Jeffries, Verandah Cottage, Vale of Health' finds you?"

"Yes."

"It brings all good wishes, of course. Being a bachelor I've had to rely on my own unaided taste. If the things don't seem very useful just at present, they will be."

In spite of his twinkle, I did not fear that his present would not be in the best of taste, and I thanked him for it, whatever it was. Then, when I returned to my own office, I found another surprise. A square, shop-packed, registered parcel lay on my desk. This, when I opened it, I found to contain a large silver cigarette-box with my name upon it, the offering of my three "Juns. Ex. Con." It was full of cigarettes of a far finer quality than any for which I had yet acquired the taste; and though only the mandarins of the F.B.C. were supposed to smoke on the premises, "Whitlock—Peddie——," I said, "have a cigarette?"

All of them appeared to come with a start out of a quite unusual absorption in their work.

"This is very good of you fellows," I said awkwardly.

The Debit Account

So we lighted up, the four of us, and with the coming of lunch-time I had to stand whiskies and soda at Stone's. I learned later that on my wedding evening all three of them got quite disinterestedly drunk in honour of the occasion.

I found on reaching home that evening that Pepper's "small parcel" was really two, the larger one about the size of an ordinary bureau, the smaller one perhaps no bigger than a tea-chest. As both were addressed to me, neither had been opened; but I really feared that this severe continence had done both Evie and her aunt an injury—so much so that I mercifully cut short my affectation of not noticing the huge packages.

"If he's not going to sit down without opening them!" cried Evie, revolted. "And a hammer and chisel put ready to his hand——!"

"Oh, these things," I said. "They're from Pepper, I suppose. Do you want them opened at once?"

"Do we want——! Open them instantly!"

"Well, I can't in here——"

I carried the boxes out into our tiny verandah-roofed yard, and there prised the lids off. Then I fell back before the onslaught they made on the straw with which the cases were filled. The smaller one contained a silver-mounted champagne-cooler; the larger one two enormous branched silver candlesticks, big enough to have furnished the table that stood before the Ark of the Covenant. So splendid were they that Evie, seeing them, did not dare to touch them; and I remember how Pepper had said that they would be useful by-and-by—which, I may say, they were.

"Hm!" I said. "Well, we'd better pawn 'em at once. We've certainly nowhere to put them."

And indeed, the objects, the cases they came in, and ourselves, almost cubically filled the little yard. Besides taking the shine completely out of the rest of the house, they cost me getting on towards a pound of candles that night, for of course we had to have another grand illumination in their honour; but Pepper only laughed when I told him.

"I'm setting you a scale of living, my boy," he said. "If you spend a lot you've got to make a lot—that's all about it."

"Well, I'll be even with you," I replied, "for your champagne-cooler's going to be my waste-paper basket."

And so it was, for long enough.

In this "setting me a scale of living" Pepper was aided and abetted by Pettinger, for if the candlesticks of the one meant the extravagance of candles, so did the two great china bowls of the other a constant expenditure of money on flowers. The only immediate profit I had of any of these magnificences was a plentiful supply of firewood. The cases they all came in, when knocked to pieces, made quite a respectable stack of timber.

There were only a couple more wedding presents that I need particularise. The first of these puzzled us for a long time. It came by letter post, a small, soft parcel addressed to Evie, containing a crochet-bordered teacloth; and except for an "L." written on a blank card, there was no indication of who the sender might be. Then I remembered Miss Levey.

"Of course—how stupid not to think of it!" said Evie. "I'll write her a note at once, and you can give it to her to-morrow."

"Oh—we'll spend a penny on it," I said.

But that very evening, before the note was posted, Miss Levey's present came, a pair of chimney ornaments—bronzed Arabs taming mettlesome steeds—brought by a young man who might have been either a cousin or a pawnbroker's assistant.

And as an explicit note accompanied the Arabs, the crochet teacloth remained unaccounted for.

And so the days slipped by. I was now unfit for anything until I should be married, and Evie was as restless as myself. A great shyness now began to come over her at times, leaving her, perhaps in the middle of a conversation, with never a word to say; and I understood, and secretly exulted. She bloomed indeed at those moments....

Let me, without losing any more time, come to the eve of my wedding and the last night I spent in my bachelor rooms.

I paced for long up and down my empty room that night. I had put on a pair of soft slippers, for the room was immediately above a dormitory where a number of shop-girls who "lived in" slept; and the light of my single candle was reflected in one or other of the squares of my naked windows as I walked. Then I threw up one of the sashes, and looked out among my terra-cotta Satans and festoons.

It was a marbled night of velvet black and iron grey, the two hues so mysteriously counterchanged that you could have fancied either to be the cloud and the other the abyss beyond until a star peeped out to tell you of your mistake. It was very still, and must have been very late, for down the road a mechanical sweeper was dragging along with a hiss of bristles. I watched it, but not out of sight, for before it had disappeared my eyes had wandered from it and were not looking at anything in particular.

I was thinking of Life—not only of that stormy share of it that up to the present had been my own, but also of that other portion of it that lay, unknown and unknowable until it should arrive, still before me. And so all my thoughts turned on the morrow as on a pivot. In nine hours or less I should be a married man, and a new time would have begun for me.

It was on the nearness of that new beginning that I brooded restlessly and passionately. For just as my Ambition had set itself the aim of that large house over Highgate way, so my Love also was going to be a thing of brightness and terraces and spires—nothing meaner, such as men shake down to out of their failure and disillusion. Ah, if care could compass it, mine was going to be a marriage! I believed that, and looking out over the Cobden Statue, I appointed that moment of our union for an expunging of all—all, all—that had gone before.

For what man old enough to have heaped up his sins does not, out of that very ache for a new beginning, seek to bespeak one of heaven by appointing a time and a season for it? Not one. Poor pathetic things of the fancy though his decrees may be, he cannot live without their expediencies. In his mind at least he sets an hour for his release.

And on that night of all nights I could not but remember all. Sins I had committed; and though some might have called that a sin which I should have proclaimed in the face of heaven to have been a righteous act, that also I remembered.... It seemed, that night, to matter little that I was acquitted of one guilt when I had incurred a wrath by other guilts innumerable; it was from the whole body of an ancient death that I fainted to be delivered. My worldly ambition I knew to be not an empty boast; oh, might but this other rebirth of mine prove to be equally well founded! A rebirth—a white page for Evie and myself to write the story of our love upon—and even that spectre of her own life, of the dreadful coming of which this was in a sense the anniversary, would not have been an agony endured for nothing! Not all in vain would have been the grim discovery of that which, four years before, had hung from a hook in a bedroom door! Not all lost, not all lost, might but the morrow prove my second natal day!

So, passionate and unresting, I prayed among my swags and emblems and gargoyles. The street-sweeper had long since gone; soon would come a lamplighter extinguishing the street lamps; now all was quiet. I dropped my head on my arms for a moment....

Then, looking up at the marbled clouds behind which the stars seemed to drift, I muttered, to Whomsoever might be up there to hear:

"Oh, let it all but sink and die away—let it all but sink and die away—and my life shall be—it shall be——"

I do not know whether my lips framed the promise of what my life should be, could I but strike my bargain.

PART II VERANDAH COTTAGE

I

In speaking of the early days of my married life I must throw myself largely on your consideration. I have not guarded through the years that sharp impatience that I presently came to feel with that tiny house in the Vale of Health. Lately I have thought more kindly of it, as if at some stage of my journey through Life (though I cannot tell when) I had heard a call behind me, turned my head, and, forgetting to turn it back again, had continued to advance backwards, recognising things in proportion as they receded. I live now in a mansion in Iddesleigh Gate; that ambition of mine, my spur in the past, is becoming a mere desire that when I go my successor shall find all in working order to his hand; and so the shabby brown earth I once trod has taken the lightsome blue of distance, and many things are seen through a sheen that, perhaps, never was there. Therefore if you would see that sheen it must be by your own favour and through whatever of glamour time and distance have given to your own young years.

For, when all allowances are made, I still think that that relation which is more than friendship was ours. Male and female (the New Man notwithstanding) we were created, and to a lower conception than that I have never in all my life declined. I have seen that declension in others, and know how it sinks ultimately to the mere comfortable security of a banking account. Whatever else I have known I have escaped that. By what wide circuit of the spirit I know not, I have returned to find the divine where others have not stirred from grossness. And I have even had glimpses of that shadowy apocalypse that finds its images, not in thrones and sceptres, but in the flesh-hooks and seething-pots of the kitchen.... But to Verandah Cottage and the Vale of Health.

I was happy with Evie, she with me. From my daily leaving her at nine o'clock in the morning until my return at half-past seven at night, she had almost, if not quite, enough to occupy her; and though I could have wished she had more friends, so that when she had finished her work the summer afternoons might not have appeared quite so long, yet I exercised a care that almost amounted to a jealousy in this regard. Understand me, however. It was against no person that I protected her with this jealous care. It was always with pleasure that I learned that Billy Izzard had looked in and talked to her for an hour at tea, or that Aunt Angela had been up to take the air or to fetch her out for a couple of hours' shopping. I merely mean that I saw no reason for her identifying herself with a set of circumstances that before long would probably have changed completely. It was part of my Ambition that, until I should have attained it, we should be a little solitary. Nor was it that I thought that the people we might by-and-by be able to meet on equal terms would be any better than those we might have known at once. It was a question of the place we were ultimately to occupy. And I begged Evie, if at times she did feel a little lonely, to be patient for my sake. So for quite a long time Billy and her aunt remained her only visitors.

The house next door might have been untenanted for all we saw of its inmates, and that, I confess, made me a little angry. I did not know the niceties of the matter, nor whether the difference between a thirty-five pound rental and one of perhaps eighty pounds outweighed those confident dicta of Evie's penny journals about "cards," "calls," and the rest; nor yet did I deem it a reason for taking anybody to my bosom that only a wall separated our dwellings; but the fact that they, whoever they were, never called stiffened me. An eighty-pound house! To put on airs about a matter of eighty pounds!... But I saw the humour of it too, and laughed.

"I'm sorry if it's rather slow, little woman," I used to say, "but wait just a bit. Let's stick it out on our own for just a little while. You'd rather be with me, now, than have waited for a year or two till we were better off, wouldn't you?"

"How absurd you are!" she would reply, nestling up to me.

"Well, keep going for a bit longer, and see what happens. I'm not deliberately hanging back from Pepper's offer for nothing, I promise you.... And at any rate the Vicar will be calling."

You see, we had agreed on the imprudence of having children at once.

But the Vicar never came, which was a fair enough hit back if he meant it for one, since we only attended his church once, and after that, I am afraid, went to churches here and there, attracted by good singing, a beautiful fabric, a man with brains preaching, and other things that perhaps mitigated the quality of our worship. And very frequently we did not go to church at all, but explored the Heath instead. And often, on Saturdays and Sundays, we went still farther afield. Greenwich had been hallowed to us by our half-day's honeymoon, and as if in this Hampton Court had suffered a slight, we made amends by going to the latter place quite often. We must have gone four or five times that summer, so that we got to know the Lelys and the Holbeins and the tea-shops, and the long drag home again from Waterloo in the old horse-bus, quite well. And one week-end we spent with Pettinger, at his place at Bedford, with two cattle-show men, an actor and an International footballer, all on their best behaviour until Evie had gone to bed. Then, when I joined her, she accused me of having had more than one glass of whisky, and wanted to know what we had been talking about all that time. I tried to tell her "the bubonic plague," but my tongue betrayed me, and I came a cropper.

So, as I had done before during our engagement, I could look up from my work during the day, past the Duke of York's Column and over the Mall, and wonder what she was doing at that moment—changing our pillow-cases, popping the pared potatoes into the saucepan of cold water, dusting, washing up, polishing, or pottering about the flower-boxes I had set on our little balcony.

The Debit Account

Miss Levey had still not been asked to come up and see Evie, but so quietly tenacious of her purpose did I divine her to be, that I was sorry I had not invited her at once and got it over. The thing was beginning to look almost like an unacknowledged contest between us. At times I forgot my original reason for keeping her at arm's-length—her forwardness, pertinacity, and racial hunger for the rags and bones and old bottles of gossip; and that she "spelt" to be asked was in itself reason enough for ignoring her hints. I may say that by doing so I cut myself from quite a distinguished circle of acquaintances, and on this point had sometimes to check my three clerks. For never a notability called on Pepper but Miss Levey, on the strength of being called in to take down in shorthand a conversation, claimed him for a close acquaintance. And as far as I can make out, she must actually have believed it, for she kept up the fiction even to us, who knew perfectly well all about it. Goodness knows what she told outsiders.... So with Whitlock, Stonor and Peddie it became a byword to say, when speaking of somebody exalted: "You know who I mean—that pal of Miss Levey's—Lord Ernest," or "Miss Levey's friend—what's his name—the President of the Board of Trade."

After the present of the silver cigarette-box, not to speak of the handsome compliment of their intoxication on my wedding night, I had thought it the least I could do to ask Whitlock and Stonor (Peddie lived out Croydon way, too far to come) to come up one Sunday and have tea with us. So they had been, and for two hours had displayed manners as highly starched as their collars. They had been, I fancy, a little surprised that, if I was a Balzac in a dressing-gown, my wife at any rate was no Sand in a flannelette peignoir. (For that matter, nothing was ever neater than Evie's skirts and blouses, and when by-and-by she began to make her own things there could hardly have been anything more becoming than her clear, sweet-pea-coloured muslins, that really would have been too rippling and Tanagra-like altogether had it not been for the stiffer petticoats beneath.) I surmised later that Stonor had taken, so to speak, a mental pattern of Evie, for matching purposes when he should come upon another girl like her; and Whitlock, whose pose it was that he would never marry, could on that very account admire the more openly.

The visit of the two clerks, of course, made my attitude towards Miss Levey all the more pointed; but I still preferred not to have her at the Vale of Health. And seeing this, Evie vowed that she did not want her either. The two Arab horse-tamers stood on our drawing-room mantelpiece, not because I admired them, but simply because we had nowhere else to put them; and they were all of Miss Levey that was absolutely needful to our happiness.

Yet I recognised that the lack, not of Miss Levey, but of company in general, was far harder on Evie than it was on me. I knew exactly why I didn't want overmuch company; Evie, who had the deprivation actually to bear, had to take the reason on trust. All my interests lay ahead; she knew only the tedium of the present. It was her part, if I may so express it, to keep bright those ridiculous empty candlesticks of Pepper's without my own certainty that candles were coming to fill them—to polish those rose bowls of Pettinger's without knowing where the roses were coming from. And I could hardly blame her if sometimes she seemed to be a little in doubt whether, after all, the things I prophesied so confidently were not merely fancy pictures of what I should like the future to be.

So, more to occupy her than anything else, I bought her out of my small earnings a hand sewing-machine, and paid for a lesson for her once a week at a skirt-maker's. And that made things rather easier. She could now pick not only her blouses to pieces, but her skirts also; and from a fear lest my interest in these occupations of hers might appear simulated when she showed me the results on my return at night, I actually did cast an eye on a costumier's or modiste's window now and then, relating to her, though goodness only knows in what masculine terms of my own, what I had seen. And during the day I could gaze past the Duke of York's Column with its wheeling pigeons and think of her, unpicking, pinning tissue-paper patterns, basting, threading the eye of her sewing-machine needle, or, with some garment or other tucked under her crumpled chin, trying to see the whole of herself at once in the narrow strip of mirror she had fetched from the bedroom.

Between Evie's happiness and my important affairs with Pepper, I do not know which was my major and which my minor preoccupation. If my Love and my Ambition were really one, that only meant that often I had to do half a thing at a time. Since Judy and I did not discuss our private affairs at the offices in Waterloo Place, it followed that we had to do so after the day's work was over; and, having been away from home all day, this sometimes caused me to absent myself for the greater part of the evening also. At first, unwilling to do this, I had brought Pepper home with me; but as he always seemed altogether too bright a jewel for our little cottage, and as Evie, moreover, besides getting flurried about what she was to give him to eat, always drew in her horns in his presence, reproaching herself afterwards that she had seemed stupid to my friend, that had not so far proved a great success. The only alternative was, that I should dine with him, getting away afterwards as soon as I could. I did not like this, but it was unavoidable.

From my observation of some at least of the hotels Pepper took me to, I judged that he had some sort of a running account, balanced afterwards, whether in cash or consideration, I knew not how; for often enough, barring the tip to the waiter, no money seemed to change hands. At other times and other places he paid what seemed to me extravagant sums. Sometimes he was in evening dress, sometimes not; I, of course, never was; and so, places where the plastron was *de rigueur* being closed to us, I did not at first see Judy in the full blaze of his splendour. On the whole, we dined most frequently at Simpson's, where morning dress is not conspicuous; and it was one night at Simpson's that Judy mentioned this very matter to me.

"By the way," he said suddenly, over his coffee, as if he had been on the point of forgetting something, "better keep a week next Wednesday free. I want you to meet Robson."

I was conscious of a sudden slight constriction somewhere inside me. Robson was not royalty, but as far as I was concerned he might almost as well have been.

"The Berkeley, at eight," Judy continued. "You'll dress, of course!"

I wondered what in. His champagne-cooler and candlesticks, perhaps....

"You needn't be afraid of Robson," Pepper continued, perhaps noticing my dismay. "As a matter of fact, he's rather afraid of me, so *you* ought to be able to pulverize him."

I saw that I must take my stand at once.

"You can bring Robson to Verandah Cottage if you like," I said shortly, "but I'm not going to the Berkeley."

"Rubbish," Pepper remarked lightly. "The table's booked. Robson's coming down from Scotland specially, and Campbell will be there too, and George Hastie. Hastie's put off a visit to Norway on purpose. You've got to tell 'em what you told me that Sunday at the Bull and Bush."

"Then if they want to hear that, they'll have to have it from you."

Pepper showed not a trace of impatience. "My dear chap, don't I just wish I *could* put it as you did!" he flattered me.... "No, no; I've told them all about you, and it's you, not me, they're coming to see.... What's the difficulty?" he asked, with a little scintillation of amusement.

"The difficulty is that if you'd told me this a week ago, I should have stopped it."

"So I thought," he replied dryly.... "Do you know West's, in Bond Street?"

The Debit Account

"No."

"Well, you'd better go there to-morrow." Then he patted my arm. "Can't be helped, Jeff. The plunge has to be taken. You won't find 'em snobs. It's the waiters you dress for—I expect that's why you dress like 'em. Good Lord, these chaps have got far too much on their minds to bother about *that*!... Go to West's and take my card; I'll 'phone 'em. I gave way to you before; if you don't give way to me now, you'll wreck us. I'd have had it at Alfred Place if I could, but I don't want Hastie and Robson there. So you go to West's to-morrow, and remember, a week on Wednesday, at eight."

I did go to West's on the morrow, and my brow grows moist yet when I think of it. It appeared that before West's could dress me they had to undress me, and my wild and half-formed thoughts that I might pass as a bushranger or miner or wealthy and eccentric antipodean vanished. Miners' flannel shirts are not patched as neatly as Evie had patched mine; bushrangers do not wear loose cuffs with gold-washed links at eighteenpence a pair; and the respectful "Sirs" to which my two acolytes treated me made my hands itch dangerously to knock their heads together.... So they ran their fingers over my burning body; and because Pepper had let me in for this, I partly, but only partly, got back at him by ordering an admirable lounge suit also, which, for all I know, he owes for to this day. Then I left that place of torture, almost prepared to think twice of my Ambition if it was going to involve very much of this kind of thing.

Evie had received the news of my approaching introduction to exalted personages with a certain wistfulness, which she had tried to cover with an extreme brightness of manner. Of course my position was altogether anomalous; that "scale of living" of Pepper's, coming far too early for my circumstances, was a white elephant; but I don't think it was that that made Evie at the same time brightly fussy and secretly shrinking. Rather, I imagine, it was that for the first time she began to fear my Ambition a little. I don't mean that hitherto she had been hoping that my great plans were baseless imaginings, but I do mean that she was settled and happy as she was, and that a Verandah Cottage twice as big would have contented her to the end of her days. When I brought that really splendid dress suit home (for I had had it sent to the F.B.C., not wishing those ducal tailors to know the poverty of my address), I think her mind suddenly enlarged to strange disturbing vistas, and she examined the stitching of the garments thoughtfully.

"They're beautifully made," she said softly. "I never saw anything finished like that. But I wish Mr Pepper had not had to pay for them."

"Pepper pay?" I laughed. "Pepper'll pay when the cows come home. It isn't that that's troubling me."

"What then?" she asked.

"I want to see you dressed like that too.... But don't you want to see me with them on?"

"Yes," she said, but as it were obediently, because I had suggested it.

I went upstairs and got into those costly garments. I had ordered shirts, and ties too, and, not being in the habit of wearing undergarments, I had to consider what to do with the small tab beneath the plastron that should have anchored me forrard. With my penknife I finally performed the operation for appendicitis upon it. Then, looking bigger even than usual, I descended, black, white and majestical.

"Your tie won't do," said Evie. "Come here."

But suddenly, as she was refashioning my bow, she flung her arms about my neck and burst into tears on my breast. Then, when I asked her gently what was the matter, she only withdrew herself, wiped her eyes, and said that she was silly. Queer creatures. It was only the newness and unfamiliarity of the prospect. It was as if she was quite happy in her poverty, merely thinking of riches....

I myself had the trifling care on my mind of who was going to sit with Evie while I lorded it at the Berkeley. Ordinarily I should have counted on her aunt, but Miss Angela had announced that she must go to Guildford that day on some business or other connected with the late Mrs Merridew's will. There was, of course, Miss Levey, but I still considered Verandah Cottage too humble for the friend of Lord Ernest and the confidante of the President of the Board of Trade. Evie protested that she would be quite all right alone, but that I would not hear of.

"I'll tell you what," I said. "Give Billy Izzard dinner that evening. I'll go round and ask him to sit with you. That'll be the best thing."

"I should be quite, quite all right, dear," she said again.

"No," I replied, "I'll get Billy. I'll write a note to him now. Then I'll show you the other suit."

The other suit did not flutter her quite so much. It was just as exquisite in its way, an iron-grey hopsack, with trousers for which I had had to peel three times, but it did not speak quite so plainly of functions and high assemblages. I really did not know where I was going to keep these two suits, as I had no trousers press, and our wardrobe accommodation was exceedingly limited; and I discovered, on arriving home early on the evening of the Berkeley dinner, that I had no summer overcoat fit for my *grande tenue*. As the choice lay between taking a cab the whole of the way and wearing my heavy winter ulster, I chose the latter alternative; and Evie tied my bow and turned up the bottoms of those trousers that pre-supposed broughams and wicker wheel-guards and alightings on red druggets under awnings built out over pavements.

"Billy'll be here in an hour," I said. "I'll look in on him as I pass. You'll be quite all right till then, and I'll be back as soon as I can. Good-bye, darling."

She stood in skirt and delaine blouse at the ivy-green, glass-panelled door, and waved her hand as I turned the corner. I sought the bus terminus in the High Street, treading carefully, for it had been raining, and there were puddles to avoid. The bus started. Twenty minutes later I got down opposite my old place with the gargoyles and terra-cotta ornaments. I mounted the stairs and tapped at Billy's door, entering as I tapped.

"Time you were starting for Verandah Cottage, Billy," I said....

The next moment I was staring open-mouthed at what was before me.

II

"All right, Louie—thanks," said Billy Izzard. "Right-o, Jeffries—I didn't think it was so late——"

But the model on the throne did not get down.

I had parted my ulster in coming up the stairs, and my dress beneath showed. The contrast struck me as brutal. For one moment I was conscious of it; I don't think that she was, even for one moment. I don't think she saw anything of me but my eyes. I did not of her.

Billy had turned his back on his work, but still she did not move. More even than my own ceremonial dress the bit of crochet woolwork that lay on the edge of the throne seemed to accentuate the drama that was all sight, with never a word spoken. As if my eyes had moved from hers, which they did not, I seemed to see the whole of that room

The Debit Account

that had been my own—the imps beyond the sills, Billy's traps, his arrangements of curtains about the four windows, the bed behind the screen where I divined her clothing to lie. I say I saw all these things without once looking at them....

The exquisite study was on the easel, and I saw that too—the thing as it was, east-lighted, admirably cool, the work of an unrepeatable two hours. Billy, I knew, would look on that canvas on the morrow as an athlete afterwards measures with astonishment his effortless jump. It was the eye's flawless understanding....

"It isn't a picture," Billy grunted over his shoulder, his fingers rattling the tubes in his box. "Where the deuce did I put that palette-knife?—Just a study—I had it in my hand not two minutes ago——"

Still she and I stood as motionless as a couple of stones.

"Dashed if I won't be methodical yet! I never—ah, here it is.... Right, Louie; I've finished. Chuck my coat over the screen, will you? Sorry, Jeff—I'd forgotten the time—but I must wash these brushes."

My eyes parted from Louie Causton's as reluctantly as a piece of soft iron parts from the end of the magnet. She moved, became alive, stepped down from the throne; and as she passed without noise to the screen I saw again, by what legerdemain of visual memory I cannot tell you, the soft flow of draperies that had always drawn my eyes as she had moved about the old Business College in Holborn.

Not until she had disappeared did I myself move from the spot I had occupied since I had taken my first two strides into the room.

"Just turn that thing with its face to the wall; I don't want to see it till morning," said Billy, bustling about. "Sha'n't be a minute——"

He dashed out with a cake of soap and a handful of brushes. The tap was on the landing below. From behind the screen came soft sounds as Miss Causton dressed....

I have wasted paper in trying to set down what my thoughts and sensations were. Not to waste any more, I will tell you instead what I did. It was some minutes later, and already the running of the tap at which Billy was washing his brushes below had ceased. Time pressed. Without quite knowing how I got there, I was standing by the screen. I spoke in a low and very hurried voice.

"Miss Causton——"

The moving of clothes stopped.

"I can't see you now—I'm late already," I said.

Miss Causton's voice had formerly been drawlingly slow, but it came back quickly enough now, and altogether without surprise.

"Yes, yes—I want to see you too—quick—how late shall you be?"

"I don't know—eleven—I can't ask you to wait——"

"I'll wait—I'll have my dinner here——"

"Where, then?"

"Where are you going?"

"Piccadilly way——"

Then, breathlessly, "Swan & Edgar's, at eleven——"

"No, no——"

"Sssh—there's no time to talk—there, at eleven——"

"Half-past ten——"

"Yes——"

The Debit Account

Billy came in again, but I was away from the screen by then. "Better hurry, unless you want a cold dinner," I said, moving towards the door; and "Better hurry yourself," I heard him say as I left....

I dashed across the road for a bus that was just starting; but it was not for some minutes after I had settled myself inside it that I began to realise what I had just done.

Then as bit by bit I grew calmer, it struck me as in the last degree remarkable. What had so suddenly impelled me to say, "I can't see you now?" And why had she replied that she too wished to see me? Why should I have wished to see her at all? Or she me? And why that long, long stare of eyes into eyes?

Robson, the Berkeley, my painfully marshalled statement, Pepper and Hastie and Campbell and all—these things had gone as completely out of my mind as if they had had no bearing at all on my life and fortunes.

I had squeezed into a corner of the bus farthest from the door, and the vehicle had glass panels forward. These were blurred with a fresh shower, orange squares, with now the halo of a lamp moving slowly past, now a muffled or umbrella-ed figure. We pulled up for a moment before the pear-shaped globes of a chemist's window, ruby and emerald, and then went forward again, and I seemed once more to hear that breathless "Swan & Edgar's—eleven," and my own "No, no!"...

I had not wanted that. I had not wanted to keep her at *that* corner, draggle-skirted, searching faces for the face she wanted, looked at in her turn, perhaps moved along by the police. For whatever I had thought before, if I had thought anything, that long union of our eyes had held no meanings of commonness....

But why the appointment at all?

"Well," I thought within myself as the bus drew up for a moment at the Adam and Eve, and then started forward again down Tottenham Court Road, "at least this explains the 'L' on the teacloth."...

After a lapse of time of which I was hardly conscious, I became aware of the glow of the Palace and the lights of Shaftesbury Avenue. By sheer force of will I dragged myself back to the present. Inexplicable as it all was, it must wait. My other business could not wait. Now for the Berkeley....

Perhaps the strange incident helped me rather than otherwise in a thing I had had quite heavily on my mind. This was the stepping out of the hansom I had picked up in the Circus and my entry into the hotel. Concerned with so much else, I had now no unconcern to rehearse. I threw my hat and coat into a pair of hands that for all I knew might not have been attached to any human body, and grunted out Pepper's name as if I had been a preoccupied monarch. I was one of twenty others who lounged or waited in the softly lighted hall, but I think the only conspicuous thing about me was my size.... Then I was aware of Pepper himself, beckoning to me across intervening heads and shoulders.

"Here he is—late as usual," he said, as if a nightly unpunctuality at such places as the Berkeley was a weakness without which I should have been an excellent fellow.

To my abstracted apology I added that not only was I late, but must leave fairly early also.

"Not unless it's for a woman," Pepper laughed. "We'll let him go then, eh, Robson? This is Jeffries—Sir Peregrine Campbell—Mr Robson. Well, let's go up. *Seniores priores*, Campbell."

We sought the private room Pepper had engaged.

The Debit Account

Even had the deep disturbance of my meeting Louie Causton face to face (if I may call it that) not banished things of less consequence, I still do not think that, socially speaking, I should have let Pepper down too badly. It was less formidable than I had feared. Robson, whom I need not describe, since you know his face from his countless photographs, had evidently, from the look of his shoulders, brushed his hair after putting his coat on; and Sir Peregrine Campbell made his vast silver beard a reason for not wearing a tie beneath it. A watch-chain or a ring apart, Hastie's and Pepper's clothes were no better than those I wore. The table was round. I was put between Pepper and Robson, and Pepper's command to a waiter, "Just take that thing away, will you?"—the thing being a centrepiece of flowers—enabled me to see Hastie and Campbell on the other side.

Pepper's tact on my behalf that night was matchless. Especially during the early part of the meal, when Robson was talking about Scotch moors, Hastie of tarpon-fishing in Florida, and Sir Peregrine (in a Scotch accent harsh as a macadam plough) of places half over the globe, he protected me (who had seen the sea only at Brighton and Southend) with such unscrupulousness and mendacity and charm that I really believe I passed as one who could have given them tale for tale had I chosen; and I gathered that he had carefully concealed my connection with the F.B.C.... "Has Jeffries shot bear?" he interrupted Hastie once, intercepting a direct question. "Look at him—he doesn't shoot 'em—he *wrestles* 'em—Siberian fashion, with a knife and a dog!... I beg pardon, Robson, I interrupted you——" And so on. He told me afterwards that my hugeness and my taciturnity had created exactly the impression he had wished. You would have rubbed your eyes had you been told, seeing me in those evening clothes, that less than four years before I had worn a commissionaire's uniform in Fleet Street and touched my cap to the proprietors of Pettinger's paper.

But until our real business should begin I took leave to drop out of the conversation more and more. That low, urgent whispering over Billy Izzard's screen ran in my head again, with the thought that I had made an inconvenient and apparently purposeless appointment for half-past ten. *Why* had that quick exchange of whispers been as it were torn out of us, and *what* had she to say to me, I to her?

Again I remembered her and her story. I remembered her cynical concealment of depth under the ruffled shallows of lazy speech, the dust it had pleased her to throw into eyes by her affectations of perverseness or indifference, her munching of sweets, her exquisite hands, her violin-like foot, her soaps and pettings of a person that even then I had divined to be ill-matched with her not strikingly pretty face. I remembered the vivid contrast between her and Kitty Windus—Kitty's ridiculous fears of non-existent dangers from men in omnibuses or under gas-lamps, and Louie Causton's nonchalant, "Men, my dear? So long since I've spoken to one I really forget what they're like!" And I remembered the event that had unstrung poor Kitty and shocked Evie once for all out of her unthinking girlhood—the news that, however it had come about, Miss Causton had one day given birth to a son. That son must be between four and five years old now....

Yet it was hardly likely she had wished to speak to me about her little boy....

And why had she sent Evie that piece of crochet as a wedding present? That too became the odder the more I thought of it. Had the teacloth been, not primarily a present to Evie, but a message to myself? The teacloth—that long, long stare—that breathless conversation over the screen—were these, all of them, calls of some sort to me?

Yet to appoint Swan & Edgar's, at half-past ten! I disliked that intensely. Not every lonely woman who has taken to herself a lover would willingly court what, were I but five minutes late, she would have to endure at that rendezvous. And the more I thought of it the more convinced I was that, not anything base, but austerity, command and a glassy clearness had lain in that long regard I had met on pushing at Billy's studio door and seeing her standing there....

The Debit Account

Then it crossed my mind that Evie was probably thinking of me that moment and wondering how I was getting along in my high company....

I could not have told you that night what the Berkeley dinners were like. I ate and spoke mechanically, and plates were taken away from me of which I had barely tasted, yet of which I had had enough. Then there came an interval without plate, or rather with a plate, doyley and finger-bowl all stacked together, and I heard Pepper say: "Let's have coffee now and then see we aren't disturbed.... Well, what about business?"

Five minutes later we were deep in the matters that were the reason of my being there.

These again Judy handled exquisitely, making of my own statement especially the most skilful of examinations-in-chief. Ostensibly laying down lines of policy himself, he contrived that these should be a drawing of me out; and it was only afterwards that I recognised how frequently he set up a falsity for me, coming heavily in, to demolish. Though ordinarily I can concentrate my thoughts when necessary for a day and a night together, I have no power of sustained speech; and so Pepper "fed" me with opportunities for destruction or approbation or comment. No large occurrence in any part of the world is immaterial to our business; as we have to look forward, reasonably probable occurrences and developments are more important still; and so our talk ranged from current events, such as Hunter's recent loss, Rundle's operations, or Loubet's plans for a *rapprochement* of the municipalities, to the coming American elections, the state of the labour world, and the health of the Queen. To the test of these general conditions, particular proposals were submitted; and though I had long known Pepper's private "hand," the skill with which he now played it was a revelation to me. At one and the same time he was laying the foundations of a dividend-paying business and of an administrative programme of which he and I were to be an indispensable part; and so, knowing more of some things than Robson, and more of others than Campbell, he set them one at another, coming in himself from time to time with an idea born of themselves five minutes before, but given back so cut and polished that it had the appearance of a new thing. I prudently said little save on an overwhelming certitude, but I think I encompassed it all and made my presence felt, now sweepingly, now as a mere deflection. I was now oblivious of all, save our conference. I seem to remember that at one juncture I must have spoken for getting on for five minutes, a feat unparalleled for me; but I knew my ground. It was of the academic Socialism and the newer kind, then just showing over the horizon, and perhaps better understood by those who like myself had gone through the fire than by any official. I was only interrupted once, by Pepper, when I mentioned Schmerveloff's name, the Russian social doctrinaire. "Ah yes, your neighbour," he murmured, and I went on....

Then suddenly I looked at my watch. It was ten minutes past ten. I still had some minutes, and I used them for a sort of cadenza to whatever my performance might have been. Then, rising abruptly, I said I must be off.

"I must be getting along myself presently," said Pepper.

He came downstairs with me and saw me into my hat and coat. I saw his glance at my new topper, but he said nothing either about my appearance or my recent demeanour. Instead it was I who said suddenly, as we walked to the door, "By the way—you didn't tell me that that neighbour of mine was Schmerveloff."

He laughed. "Didn't I? Well, you ought to know who your neighbour is better than I do!" It was only then that he added, "Well, I think we've done the trick, Jeffries!"

I left him, and turned towards Swan & Edgar's. I had another trick to do now, though of what its nature might prove to be I had not the faintest conception.

III

As they had done three hours before, again our eyes met simultaneously. She had been sheltering in a doorway, but she advanced immediately, and without hesitation took my arm. I suppose she must have chosen our direction, for we had crossed to the corner of Lower Regent Street before I had as much as wondered where, at that hour of the night, we were to go. It was still raining; the flimsy umbrella she carried protected her soft grey hat, but not her skirts; and I did not wish to take her to any of the brightly lighted establishments of the Circus for two reasons—first, because I had only four shillings in my pocket, and secondly, because I wanted—well, say to distinguish. The west-bound buses start from the corner to which we had crossed, and it looked as if we should have to talk in whichever of them took her homewards.

"This one?" I said laconically, as a West Kensington bus drew up.

But she drew me away. "Let's go this way," she said.

I took her umbrella, and with her hand still on my arm she led me down Lower Regent Street.

If we had anything important to say to one another, it was extraordinary how we delayed to say it. We reached the offices of the F.B.C. without having spoken, and turned along Pall Mall East and into Trafalgar Square still without a word. And when presently she did speak, at the top of Parliament Street, it was merely to tell me that my hat would be spoiled if I didn't take my share of the umbrella.

"Then you might at least turn your trousers up," she added, as I made no reply; and I stooped and did so. We resumed our walk, stopped at the Horse Guards, and made our way slowly towards the Mall.

"Are you warm?" I asked some minutes later.

"Quite," she replied; and the silence fell on us again.

At last, somewhere near the spot where the Artillery Memorial now is, she did speak. It was a curious question she put, her fingers working slightly on my sleeve as she did so. During the past minutes a sense—I hardly know how to describe it except as a sense of protection—had begun to grow on me, the odd thing being that it was not I who protected her, but she me. Perhaps the perfect calm with which she had claimed my arm had begun it; it certainly now informed the very curious question she suddenly put.

"Are you happy?" she asked.

You may imagine I was a little surprised. Quite apart from the nameless reassurance that thrilled in her tone, some queer gage of fidelity, though fidelity to what I could not make out, the question itself was a long way out of the ordinary. Was I happy! Ought I not, from any point of view she could possibly have, to be happy? Newly married—sure of myself—wearing clothes the luxury of which was only an anticipation—fresh from a conference with the great ones of the land (though to be sure she could hardly know all this)—what else should I be but happy? It looked as if for some reason or other she had supposed I would *not* be happy.... I spoke slowly.

"I wish you would tell me," I said, "what makes you ask that?"

She looked straight before her through the rain. "Why I ask that? It's just that that I wanted to ask you," she replied.

"It's just that that you——" I repeated after her, stopping, however, half-way.

Yet I felt somehow that that she had just uttered was no banal compliment. She was not thinking of the kind of felicitation that had been implied when she had sent Evie the teacloth. She had not asked after Evie, and was not, I knew already, thinking of Evie. And again I had that odd sense that she was protecting me, and would continue to protect me.

"Well, it's an odd question—the whole thing's odd, of course—but since you ask, I don't mind telling you. I am happy."

She turned under the umbrella eagerly, almost (I thought) joyously.

"You *are*?"

"*I* am," I emphasised slightly.

But still she did not mention Evie. Again we walked. Then:

"You are? After all—that?"

Softly from the background of my memory there came forward what I conceived to be her meaning. It was a humiliating one, and I hung my head humbly.

"You mean after—poor Kitty?"

But it seemed I was quite wrong. "No, I don't mean that," she said. "Or at any rate only partly that."

"Then," I asked quickly, "will you tell me what you *do* mean?"

In Billy's studio we had been positively straining at one another to speak; since then, free any time this last half-hour to say what we would, we had hung just as desperately back; but now came a sudden enough end both to straining and to reluctance. She turned to me; my eyes would have fallen before the gaze she gave me, but were compelled to endure it; and the lightning is not more instantaneous and direct than were the words that now burst from her.

"Tell me—you killed that boy, didn't you?"

I said you should have it soon. It has been a little longer than I thought. At any rate you have it now.

The remaining events of that evening are easier to set down than to account for. My difficulty perhaps is that I am trying to tell an extraordinary thing in terms that are inappropriately plain. Nothing, for example, would be simpler than to say how we stopped in our walk, presently resumed it, slowly passed the Palace and the Royal Mews, and in course of time found ourselves walking up Grosvenor Place. It is true that we did these things, but it is also true that they are all more or less beside the mark. I need not urge my point, how beside the mark they are, by comparison with the remarkable results of being asked by a woman whom you have known only slightly and whom you have almost forgotten all about whether you have killed a certain young man. Therefore if, as may very well be the case, you yourself have no experience on such a point, that is all the more reason why you should trust me to give, in my own way, the essence of an hour without parallel in my experience, and, I imagine, to be matched in that of few others.

As she had spoken I had stepped back, without haste, a pace from her, taking her umbrella with me. I was stepping back another pace, when my back encountered the iron railings, stopping me. Until then her hand had not left my sleeve. Now perhaps three yards separated us, she standing in the rain, I with her gimcrack of an umbrella. There was a lamp not far away; the veil of falling rain held and diffused the light of it, so that I

The Debit Account

actually saw her with more evenness of detail than I should have done had she stood directly in the light, one side of her face illumined, and the other dark; and probably my own face was not entirely lost in the shadow of the umbrella. Our eyes had met again, exactly as they had met in the studio....

On her soft floppy hat and over the shoulders of her three-quarters grey coat I saw the rime of fine rain gather. It became a sort of soft moss of rain, that gave her figure a faintly discerned outline of light. Though her wrists were damp and dark, and her skirts straight and heavy, I still did not think of passing her the umbrella; it is wonderful how many small things escape you when you have just been asked whether you have put an end to a young man's life. The rain came on still more sharply. I saw it gleam on the backs of her kid gloves....

It never occurred to me to wonder how she knew. I suppose I ought to have wondered this, but I gave it no thought. Instead, I was wondering why I had never noticed before what her eyes were like—why, indeed, I had thought them to be quite different. Had you asked me that morning what Louie Causton's eyes were like I should first have rummaged in my memory for who Louie Causton was, then have dismissed them as ordinary and a sort of grey, and so have missed a wonder. Grey? Yes, they were grey, but that is not saying anything. And perhaps after all it was not the eyes that held me. Perhaps the eyes were no more than rounds of crystal between us, pure crystal, hiding nothing. Better still, perhaps they were of that substance which, placed across itself, allows no light to pass, but, turned parallel, ceases to intercept. Formerly I had seen those tourmaline rounds of Louie Causton's grey eyes as it were transversely placed, opaque, riddling, mocking, impenetrable; now, quicker than the flicker of a camera-shutter, they had changed, and, for me, would never again change back. I had seen down into her soul. Her physical form, three hours before, had not been more openly offered to my gazing than was that measureless deep interior she showed me now....

And that she too had plunged to the bottom of my own soul, her question was sufficient evidence.

And now, as that vision of her spirit, stark and piercing as Billy Izzard's of her body had been, must abide with me for ever, there was no special need for hurrying matters. Though I had known it not, it was for that last stripping look that I had whispered so breathlessly to her over the screen; and she, unlike me, had known why she had whispered back. So, the thing being now done, our time was our own. As slowly as I had retreated to the railings, I advanced from them again. Once more I held the umbrella over her.

"Come," I said. "You're getting wet."

Again, without a moment's hesitation, she passed her hand under my arm, and we moved towards the Palace.

There are some supreme moments—they say the moment of violent death is one of them—in which all Life's obscurations are made instantaneously clear; but if my own supreme moment ought to have taken that form, I can only say that it did not. No sudden explanations of the hitherto inexplicable flashed through my mind. Afterwards, when a certain amount of imperfection had supervened between me and that perfect look, these explanations did present themselves, yes, in crowds, but not then. I did not ask why, knowing me for a murderer, she should still take my arm. I did not wonder how she regarded the matter from Merridew's point of view. I did not trouble myself about how she knew, nor, for the matter of that, whether she did know—for she had made no charge, had only put a question. I cared for nothing but that sweet yet terrible depth and stillness I had seen beyond the tourmalines of her eyes. Indeed, somewhere near the Palace, I suddenly found myself irresistibly longing to look into those eyes again. We were approaching another lamp. I stopped. Again I did not notice that I did so under a dripping plane-tree. I looked. They were still the same—flawless transmitters, accesses to the ether of her soul....

Again she put her question.

"You did kill that boy, didn't you?"

"Yes." (I could not have dared to lie to her.)

"Ah!"...

We walked on again.

And I know not what rest, akin to the longing of a weary spirit for death, I found in it all. Nor do I know whence came the special and unimaginable peace that filled me. For that peace was special. My marriage had been a different rapture; the dreams of the first days of my love had not been the same; and it was perhaps this that I had implored in vain that night when, stretching out among my swags and gargoyles, I had cried to Whatever lay beyond the marbled sky that, might I but be delivered from this body of an ancient death, my life should be a dedicated thing. And now, when I least expected it, I had it. Between me, a man who had committed murder, and her, the mother of a nameless child, something I knew not—something still and splendid and awful—had come into being. Do you wonder that, in the stillness and splendour and awe of it, my brain slumbered within me, so that though those grey abysses full of answers waited for me, not a question did I put?...

"Yes," I said. "You know I killed him."

And "Ah!" she said again.

You will not find it difficult to believe that when you have been asked the question I had been asked, you and your questioner are not on ordinary terms. Indeed—believe me—you are hardly flesh and blood at all. You become eyes and voices, and yet not exactly that either—you are parts of an immanent vision and speech. You will also see that to dare such a question is to dare to be questioned in your turn. Therefore, less as wanting the information than as doing her the reciprocal honour of putting her on the same stark footing as myself, I again sought those marvellous eyes.

"You asked me," I said, "whether I was happy. I told you.... Are you?"

You have learned what she was; to what you already know I will add one or two things I picked up later. I wish to show you what elements she had to make happiness out of. She did fairly well out of her sittings. Ordinarily she made as much as two pounds a week, and she made more still when she was engaged for an evening class. To this were to be added the small sums she made by her crochet-work during her short rests. (Evie's teacloth had been made during the rests.) When she did not crochet, she made garments for her boy. She rose daily at seven, dressed her boy, breakfasted with him, and at nine o'clock brought him out with her. They walked a quarter of a mile together to her bus, where the child was met each day by a guardian, an old governess she trusted. She kissed him, and blew him another kiss as the bus turned the corner. He always waited with the old governess for this, but sometimes other buses intervened, so that she went without her last glimpse of him. Then she sought the studio where she happened to be engaged. There she posed, crocheted, posed again, lunched, and once more posed. She usually reached home again at eight o'clock, but when she secured evening sittings it was eleven before she got back. By that time her boy was in bed. She dressed him well, fed him well, told him tales, and bought him tops and toy soldiers. She paid the governess ten shillings a week. Sundays were her heavenly days. If they were cold or wet, she spent them in playing with the tops and soldiers on the floor; if they were fine she took him out on to the commons of Clapham or Wandsworth, or to the Zoo, for which her employers gave her Sunday tickets. She had saved a few pounds, and was adding to this sum by shillings

The Debit Account

and half-crowns, against the day when she would have to send him to school and start him in the world. This was her life.

And when I asked her if she was happy, she said, in a voice little above a whisper, "Yes—now."

Then, with another deep, clear look, she added, "I think I have all the best of Life."

It did not occur to me just then to wonder what she meant by that "now." I was pondering her last words. All at once, on a sudden impulse (though I was pretty sure beforehand what her answer would be), I said:

"He left you?"

Her answer was supremely tranquil and unaffected.

"Yes—as far as he was ever there to leave. It meant nothing—a folly—merely stupid—it had no significance whatever. I've no grudge against him. He didn't really wrong me. It hardly mattered, ever—it doesn't matter—now——"

A question must have shown in my eyes even as I decided not to put it, for all at once she laughed a little.

"Oh, I'd tell you if you wished to know, but you'd be no wiser. It's a name you've never heard. But one thing I should like——" For one moment she hesitated.

"I ask you nothing."

"No; but I should like you to know one thing—oh, quite for my own sake! If ever you *should* hear a name—three names—four—you needn't believe them. I lied perfectly recklessly. It seemed to me—stupidly perhaps—that I owed him that. So I blackened myself. You see, they tried to find out—my friends——"

"You mean——?"

"Oh, one lover was enough," she answered, with another laugh, rich, low, and without bitterness. "And it doesn't matter—*now*."

It was then that I knew what she meant by that reiterated "now." The thing that beat suddenly in on me explained in a flash that curious attitude of protection towards myself. That kiss blown from the top of the morning bus—the shillings she earned by sitting to morose and impatient artists—those heavenly Sundays—that desertion which also she ranked as a happiness—her self-slanders rather than betray her betrayer—all these things together had not, somehow, seemed to me to make up that "best part of Life" of which she spoke. Beyond even her beautiful devotion to her boy must lie some other deep sustaining dream. Without such a dream, her life would not have been what patently it was—full....

But now it was all in the eyes she turned on me....

And I knew that the look that told me she loved *me*, had long loved me, and must now go on loving me to the end, put love between us high out of our reach for ever.

"You can't prevent it," she almost triumphed, shining it all out on me. "It's mine, whether you want me to have it or not. And of course it makes no difference to you——"

"None," I murmured mechanically....

"Then *haven't* I all the best of Life?" she exulted, smiling up at me.

And before that strange tension that for so long had held us had quite left us, I had muttered, with a little choke, "God bless your little chap, anyway!"

It was all I could say. The other thing she had told me could make no difference to me.

Then came the swift change. It came as we reached the top of Grosvenor Place, turned, and descended again. It came as a torrent of rapid speech, sometimes both of us speaking at once, both stopping and waiting, and then both breaking out simultaneously as before. They were short, half sentences, taken and given back with bewildering quickness.

"And now you want to know——" she said.

"Yes——?"

"——how I knew?"

"How did you?"

"I didn't—quite—I knew in myself—not otherwise."

"In yourself—how?"

"Oh, how does one know these things? One sees this—hears that——"

I clutched at her hand.

"Not so quickly. What 'this'? What 'that'?"

"Well, for one thing, Kitty Windus——"

"Does she know?"

"No——"

"You hesitate."

"She doesn't know. She helped me to knowledge. She doesn't know she did."

Again I snatched at her hand.

"That's not the same thing. She may know of—that other—but not know she's let you know."

"That's just possible. That's why I——"

"Oh, anything's possible!" I broke out. "Let's be plain. Does she know that I killed——?"

"I don't think so. Indeed I'll say no."

"But you hesitate again. (Come this way—it's quieter.)"

As if a fusillade had been suspended there came a thrilling silence. We were passing St. Peter's Church at the east end of Eaton Square. We were in the Square before she replied.

"Very well. Don't interrupt unless I ask you questions. I'll be as plain as I can. It's extraordinarily difficult...."

I waited.

"You see," she began carefully, "Kitty's so—queer. You couldn't expect that insane arrangement with her to go on indefinitely—I mean that incredible engagement of yours. She was bound to find out something. She——"

"Yes—that's it—what *did* she find out?" broke once more from me.

"Sssh!... Of course she found out—about Evie—that it was Evie you were in love with. Naturally she did. What woman wouldn't? *I* saw it, with far less reason than Kitty had. We won't waste time over that. So after she left you, she expected week by week to hear of the next thing—your becoming engaged to Evie. Week by week, I say. How many weeks was it?"

"Four years."

"Week by week, for four years. All those weeks. If it didn't come one week it would be the next—you see. She prophesied it. It became an *idée fixe*. You never saw her during that time?"

"I never as much as——"

"Nor heard of her?"

"No."

"You didn't hear of her breakdown?"

"No; but all this doesn't——"

"Doesn't go beyond you and Evie. I know. Don't interrupt. And Evie didn't hear of her breakdown either?"

"No—I think I can say that."

"What did Evie think of—let us say Archie Merridew's suicide?"

I hesitated. "What should she think? She thought what everybody thought—more or less."

"As something inexplicable?"

"I assume so—but of course I've never——"

"What does she think now?"

"I hope she doesn't think of it at all. As far as I've been able——"

"Yes, yes, yes.... Plainly, then, have you told her? Told her what you did?"

"Told her? No!"

"Have you *thought* of telling her?"

"Have I thought ... do you mean have I thought of killing her too?"

Louie was suddenly silent. A hansom slipped swiftly through the deserted Square, its wheels making no sound and the slap of the horse's hoofs dying gradually away in the distance. The rain had stopped, but the trees still dripped sadly, and something vague and far away had approached, resolved itself into a policeman's shining cape, and passed again before Louie spoke.

"Well," she said slowly, "after all, that's not the immediate point. That comes later. The first thing's Kitty's condition. That condition, as far as I can make it out, is this. You showed yourself clever and unscrupulous almost beyond belief in one thing, and she found you out in that; now, I fancy, she thinks there's no end to your cleverness and unscrupulousness. Positively no end. You're *capable de tout*.... So she broods. Of course she ought never to have been allowed to live alone.... And she knows she has these—fancies—about you—and so when she's all right she's quite persuaded they *are* fancies. And most of the time she *is* all right. Then the fits come, and—she's off."

A quick shiver took me. "Do you mean——?" I faltered.

"Violently? Oh no. At the best she's just as she used to be; at the worst she's merely helpless, a child. Otherwise I should never dare to have her come and live with me."

"What, you're——?"

"Well, somebody's got to look after her."

"And so you——?"

"She's coming to me next week."

"I see," I said slowly....

Again such a silence fell on us as, after prolonged sound, has an importunate quality that even sound has not. As if in a dream, I strove to realise that Evie and Billy Izzard were away over in the Vale of Health, dozing probably, awaiting my return from the Berkeley. I tried to understand the plain fact that I was walking the wet streets in the company of a woman who, judged by ordinary standards, bore a smirched reputation, and that I had permitted that woman to make, though without words, a declaration of her love for me. As this last grew on me a little, I let my mind take that particular bypath of speculation. I almost forgot her presence by my side in my odds and ends of memories of her. Once, at a breaking-up party at the old Business College, she had said to me: "As you don't come to me, I come to you," and at the same party she had asked me for a cup of coffee, which I had brought to her in the crowded room instead of giving it to her in some sequestered corner where we could "sit out." Then other memories came. Memory adding itself to memory until I had all the leading facts of her story—that fatal, insignificant, desperate accident—then, mockingly too late, her love for myself—her so strangely happy life, its fulness now to be turned into a superabundance by her voluntary taking up the care of a weak-minded woman—all, all her happy-unhappy story. And now for us to be thrown together like this! Extraordinary, extraordinary! I fancy we were somewhere in the neighbourhood of Sloane Square by this time—Sloane Square, with Evie and Billy waiting for me in the Vale of Health, and her boy asleep many hours ago!... I smiled, though grimly enough, as my eyes encountered my own trousers. Those expensive garments were soaked to the knees. Louie, broken by her day's arduous sitting, now hung heavily on my arm. Her sleeves lay flat to her arms, and her skirt held pounds' weight of water. And we were still walking down Lower Sloane Street, and approaching the Barracks....

It was in Lower Sloane Street—there is a little naturalist's shop thereabouts—that I stopped, once more facing her. It seemed to me that there was something which, if she didn't know it, she ought to know.

"Louie," I said slowly, putting a hand on her shoulder to turn her face towards mine, "I don't know whether you know what you ought to do?"

I saw that she did know. For the first time I saw a return of her old ironical smile. But "What's that?" she asked.

"What, unless you do to me, I can now equally do to you."

"And what's that?" she smiled.

"There are no accessories in this business. You're a principal too."

She laughed outright. "All right, Jim," she said. "I'll trust you not to give me away."

"But listen to me——"

That was exactly what she would not do. She cut in brusquely.

"Oh, my good man, be quiet! Anybody'd think you thought I was going to blackmail you!" Then, leaning heavily on me once more, "I suppose all you men take that view of it," she went on, with an energy that triumphed momentarily over her fatigue, "but here's *my* view if you must have it—that men deserve rewards who stamp out creatures like that! Oh, you needn't look at me—*I'm* experienced if anybody is, and *I* know why young men hang themselves just before their weddings! And that, Jim—come along, it's no good standing here—that's why I asked you whether you'd told Evie. You know your own business best, but I'll tell you this—that if women were on juries not a jury in the land would convict you! *Oh!*——" She shuddered the more strongly that she earned her daily bread in the way she did. "*I* can face these things. I've learned—I've had to. Am I the same woman you once knew? I think not. And I tell you plainly, that if you'd done what you have done for me I'd kiss your feet and ask you to bless me! But of course there's Evie. I don't know why you haven't told her: I don't know her very well, you see. My own opinion is that you'll find you've got to tell her. I'm sure that sooner or later you'll find that. And that reminds me of something else. What do you suppose you ought to do about Kitty?"

I smothered a groan. "Oh, I'm past supposing," I answered dully.

"Poor man!... Well, this is how it is. Kitty's unreliable. She has these outbreaks. I hope she'll be better with me, but I can't answer for that. So—I'm only preparing you, Jim, but

The Debit Account

it *may* come to this, that before she gets it fixed in her head once for all that young Merridew *didn't* hang himself she's got to be made quite certain that he *did*. Even if she's got to be told so she must be made certain of that. And I shall be greatly surprised if you haven't to tell Evie exactly the opposite. *Voilà!*"

I scarcely heard her now. An overwhelming weariness had come over me. It was a weariness of the mind no less than of the body. My mind too seemed to be making an endless pilgrimage through wet and benighted streets, far from its rest; and even that strange hallucination of Louie's protection had left me now. After leaving Lower Sloane Street I suppose we must have turned still farther west, for I seem to remember that we passed the Chelsea Hospital, but in this I may be wrong, unless they have since pulled down a row of old houses I distinctly remember seeing across the road. It must have been not very far from there that I went for a time, physically and mentally, all to pieces. Probably the net result of all this talk had just begun to sink into me—that, the intervening years notwithstanding—my well-nigh flawless planning notwithstanding—my cares and prayers and vigils notwithstanding—all was not yet over. I have boasted in my time that I have been untroubled by what I had done, and that is also no lie; but the consequences are another matter. Suppose even that Louie were right, and that I had done nothing but a worthy act; there are still worthy acts that overwhelm the doer of them. So the prophets were hounded to their death—and I was no prophet, but, for a space of time of which I took no account, a broken man, who, in a doorway somewhere near Swan Walk (it was an old doorway, with a porter's grille and an antique bell-rod), gave out utterly, began to double at the knees, and would have fallen but for the two arms of a woman as spent as himself—a woman who murmured, with unthinkable selflessness and a charity and encouragement and comfort past telling: "Oh, come, come—come, come!"...

By-and-by—it could not have lasted very long, for a clock somewhere was striking one, and the public-houses had been closing as we had left Sloane Square—I was better. I was well enough to walk, still supported by her, to a bench on the Embankment, where we sat down. Her umbrella was still in my hands; how I had come to break it I didn't know; but I had broken it, and I remember thinking dully, as if it had been a great matter, that I ought to get her another ... or get that one mended.... It was only right that I should pay for it. Somebody would have to pay for it, and in common fairness it ought not to be she.... And, I thought, while I was about it, I might as well get her a cab also. She must be unspeakably tired, and I had four shillings in my pocket....

"Thanks," I said. She had taken off my ruined silk hat and unfastened my white bow and collar, and was bending over me solicitously, fanning my face ineffectually, now with my own hat, now with her hand. "Thanks. That was absurd of me. I'm not—not in the habit of giving out like this—but we'll finish—another time, if you don't mind. Where do you live?"

She lived near Clapham Junction. "But what about you?" she said, as we rose.

"Oh, I'll take a cab too. I'll walk a little way though. Up here—this seems a likely place for cabs——"

We took one of the minor streets that led to the King's Road. There I hailed a hansom that was returning eastwards. I had put her into it when a thought struck me.

"By the way," I said, "what is your name—your business name, I mean?"

She smiled, as if at a wasted care. "Oh, the same," she said.

"Does Billy Izzard know you know me?"

"No. That is, he didn't."

"Well, he does by this time probably. If Evie and he have been talking——"

The Debit Account

("'Urry up, gov'nor!" growled the cabman.)

"He'll think it odd I didn't speak to you. Never mind. Where can I hear from you?"

"Your office——?"

"Yes—no, I mean, not there." I had suddenly remembered Miss Levey. "Give me your address."

She gave it to me, and I gave it to the cabman. "You really will take a cab?" she said, looking anxiously at me as the vehicle pivoted round.

"Yes, yes."

And she was off.

I was in the King's Road, without a penny. It was a quarter to two when I passed the Post Office near Sloane Square, and it was twenty past by the time I reached Park Lane. After Park Lane I lost count of the time. I came out of the doze in which I walked to find myself at various times in Upper Baker Street, near Lords, and, I don't know how long after that, on the point of missing the turning into Fitzjohns Avenue. The day began to break greyly. I still walked, sleeping as I went. It was only as I ascended Heath Street, hardly a quarter of a mile from home, that I came sufficiently out of my torpor to begin to wonder what account I should give of my absence to Evie.

FOOTNOTE:

See "In Accordance with the Evidence."

IV

Three weeks or a month after that night on which I had reopened, so to speak, a bottle containing a grim and familiar genie, an incident happened that riled me exceedingly. This was nothing less than an unexpected meeting, on one of our Sunday visits to Hampton Court, with Miss Levey.

Under other circumstances this meeting would have been too ludicrous for annoyance. It happened in the Maze, of all places, where, in some moment of physiological high spirits, I had taken Evie, threatening to lose her and leave her there. As a matter of fact, I had lost both her and myself. Perhaps you know the Maze. Its baffling windings of eight-foot hedges have their single legitimate way out, which you may find if you can; but, for the release of burrowers at turning-out time, there is also a locked iron gate, as impossible to miss as the true exit is to find. Half-a-dozen times, believing ourselves to be at last in the proper alley of green, we had been brought up by this gate; and it was at the gate that we met Miss Levey.

At certain points, where the high mattress-like hedges are a little thin, you can almost see through them; and several times we had caught sight of a scarlet shadow, accompanied by a young man in checks. Now, at the gate, we came full tilt upon this scarlet. Her wide hat and buttons only were black, and from her bosom projected an enormous frill, very white against the red cloth, that gave her the appearance of a pouter pigeon. She had lost Lord Ernest or the President of the Board of Trade or whoever her companion was, and of course there was no avoiding her.

The Debit Account

"*You* here!" she cried, seizing both Evie's hands and setting her head so far back and on one side that it was half lost behind the frill. "Vell!" (I write it so, though her accent was in reality less marked.) "This *is* delightful!—You see, Mr Jeffries——!"

I was mortified, but couldn't very well show it. I laughed. "Oh! What do I see?"

"Dear Evie and I do meet after all!" she half jested.

"Oh!" I laughed again. "Well, if that's all, you could have met long ago. I assumed that you didn't come up to see us because you didn't want to."

It was, of course, lame in the extreme, but Miss Levey saw fit to affect to believe it. Again she put her head back like an inquisitive bird, dandling Evie's hands up and down.

"Oh, *I* thought I wasn't wanted! So of course I stayed away.... Vell, Evie, I *am* glad!"

So Evie said she was glad, and I said that I was glad too, with something about the ridiculousness of such old acquaintances standing on ceremony, and Miss Levey, I knew, was the only glad one of the three.

"Isn't it annoying, the way we always find ourselves at this gate!" she said, when at last she had dropped Evie's hands. "Aschael and I have been here at least ten times! You ought to know the way out, Mr Jeffries, a clever man like you!"

"I'm afraid I don't, but there's the man up the perch there—he'll always point out the way."

"Oh, but one doesn't like to be beaten!" she said, with a covert look at me. "Dear me, I'm quite hot! I think Aschael must have given me the slip. Perhaps you wouldn't mind finding him for me, Mr Jeffries?"

My polite "With pleasure" didn't in the least represent my feelings, but as I thought I should recognise the pawnbroker's assistant who had brought our Arab horse-tamers, I bade them stay where they were, and left them.

After I had found the ringleted Aschael it took us half-an-hour to escape from the pair of them, and even then it was done only at the cost of the invitation I had so obstinately withheld. Miss Levey was to come up with me from the F.B.C. on the following Wednesday evening, and Aschael was to fetch her away again at ten o'clock. It seemed quite a nicely balanced point whether she would kiss Evie or not when she left, but she did not, and for some minutes after we had lost sight of them I saw the man up the perch pointing out turnings and heard his calling to them.

"Deuce take her!" I muttered, twenty minutes later, when Evie and I had also been shown the way out. We had passed the glowing parterre, and were just turning into the cool Fountain Court.

"It couldn't be helped, dear," said Evie. "It was all there was to do. We needn't get into the habit of asking her if you don't want her."

"Oh, it doesn't matter," I answered absently. I was once more wondering whether Pepper intended to take Miss Levey over presently from the F.B.C. Already I was pretty well resolved that he should not.

And I was quite resolved on this point when Evie next spoke. We had stopped by one of the arches, and were looking over the grass plot and fountain in the middle. The Court was deliciously cool, and I should have liked Billy Izzard to make a sketch of Evie as she leaned against the pillar, dressed in soft pink muslin, her hand touching her cheek, and only her dark eyes darker than that Black Knight sweet-pea of her hair. Those eyes were full of grave thought.

"Jeff," she said diffidently by-and-by.

"What, dear?"

"You know where you left us just now——"

"Left you and Miss Levey?"

"Yes.... She told me something I think I ought to tell you."

"Oh? She didn't lose much time," I could not forbear remarking.

"It was something I know you'd far rather I told you—it was something about poor Kitty," Evie went awkwardly on.

"Oh?"...

You may guess from this "Oh?" that I had told Evie no more than I had thought fit about my meeting with Louie. Indeed, of that extraordinary walk that had begun at Swan & Edgar's corner and ended in the King's Road, Chelsea, I had told her nothing at all. When I had reached home again, at four o'clock in the morning, Evie had been in bed, Billy asleep by the ashes of the dining-room fire. He had yawned hugely and stiffly: "A-a-a-h!... I like your idea of a couple of hours in the evening, my friend! I say, you look rather done up; what have you been doing with yourself?... Evie? She went to bed at two; she would sit up till then. What time is it? Nice goings-on at the Berkeley!"

And Billy and I had lighted the fire and breakfasted, moving about quietly so as not to wake Evie. Evie did not know the exact hour of my return, and had made no remark about the condition of my hat and trousers.

It seems an odd thing to say, but I simply had not dared to tell her. When I say that she would never, never have understood I am not belittling her either; she simply would not have understood. It would have been different had I been able to tell her all, but better nothing than half. Nay, what she already knew was in its way almost too much, for of course Billy, taking studio mysteries for granted, had told her, rather as a joke against myself, of my coming upon Louie Causton. Seeing Evie's almost painful blush, he had been a little sorry he had spoken. For while Evie liked Billy, she could never get used to the idea of his models. It was a little as if some outwardly very charming person should be in reality a known dynamiter. And even when she had grasped the model (so to speak) in theory, it had only to be made a personal matter for the blood to rise into her cheeks. Suppose I had come upon Aunt Angela thus!... So, unable to tell her all, of the later events I had told her nothing.

But now she said again, looking over the quiet Fountain Court, "It's about poor Kitty. Louie didn't tell you, I suppose?" (I had admitted having had a few words with Louie.)

"In Billy's studio, do you mean?"

"Yes."

"No," I answered, with what strictness of veracity you will observe.

I saw, by the way she dropped her great eyes and pushed a bit of gravel about with her toe, what had come over her again. Just as, on that Bank Holiday evening in the tea-garden in the Vale of Health, she had had Kitty, if not on her conscience, at any rate on her magnanimity, so she had her now. By reason of that slight emptiness and waiting state of her life (in spite of all that I could do), her thoughts still flew back. Between my departures in the mornings and returns again o' nights, reminiscences, the freer in their play that her work was merely mechanical, still occupied her. These reminiscences welled up again in her now, and, added to them, filling her breast completely, was that half-compunctious desire of the victress for the squaring of accounts that is to be found in the exercise of compassion.

And as I saw her perturbation, something welled up in me too. She did not know I was looking at her, but I was, and already I had begun to see the only thing that would be more than temporarily efficacious against these strayings. There was only one thing. A

The Debit Account

picture came into my mind of a woman who blew a kiss from the top of a bus, played on the floor on Sundays with her boy, and found her life full and happy....

"Oh, my darling," I thought as I looked at her, "is it so very, very long—so very long and empty?... Very well.... It will modify a good many plans, but better that.... Your life too shall be full—and your arms——"

When next she looked up there was, about her eyes, a tiny bright edging of tears that did not fall.

"Jeff," she said, unusually quickly, "Kitty's ill. She has attacks of some kind. I couldn't quite make it out. I suppose Miriam Levey'll tell us all about it on Wednesday. I know you don't like Miriam, but she's awfully troubled about Kitty, and thinks she ought to be looked after. Somebody told her—told Miriam—that poor Kitty'd been found one night walking round and round Lincolns Inn Fields, and when the policeman asked her, she couldn't remember at first where she lived. Oh, Jeff, it does seem so sad!"

Privately I found that horrible. It had been in Lincolns Inn Fields that Kitty and I had walked together, and to think of her still haunting the place, alone, I found very horrible. But if that horror was mine, it was not going to be Evie's if I could help it. I nodded gravely, and took her arm.

"Well," I said (although I was again cudgelling my brains to see how Miss Levey's visit could be frustrated), "no doubt you will hear all about it next Wednesday. I wouldn't worry till then.... What about tea?"

We left the Palace, and sought the teashop near the Bridge. Miss Levey and Aschael passed the door of the shop as we sat, and Miss Levey waved her hand and gave us an artificially bright smile. But her goose was cooked with Jeffries & Pepper. I had far too much respect for her inquisitiveness and persistence to admit her to our new enterprise. Between her and myself Pepper would not hesitate for long, and I intended, if necessary, to put the matter in precisely that form....

After tea, Evie and I took another turn in the Palace. It was a golden evening, with a wonderful bloom on the old walls, windows flashing yellow, and the forests of twisted chimney-stacks brightly gilded. Her arm was in mine, and her hand made little delicious pressures from time to time, and ever and again her cheek seemed to be on the point of falling against my shoulder. Louie Causton's touch had not thrilled me thus. Some high forbiddance would ever have said Louie Causton and myself Nay, but here was flesh of my flesh, and the promise of sweet and rosy flesh between us—for we had spoken of it, and the west that bathed all in golden light was not more tranquil than that other heaven in our hearts....

I remember very well our journey back from Waterloo in the old horse-bus that night. I remember it because of that whispered new pact between Evie and myself. She, tired out no less by that gentle vista than by the fatigues of the day, slept for the greater part of the way with her head on my shoulder and her hat in my lap; and I had to wake her to change buses. In the new bus she settled down again; and I was left free to consider whether the promise I had passed would or would not necessitate a hastening of matters with Pepper. If it should turn out so, so much the worse. In any case it had to be done. For fear of the seven devils, Evie's mind was no longer going to be left as it now was, swept and garnished.

As it happened, I was spared the trouble, though not the subsequent responsibility, of putting Miss Levey off for the following Wednesday evening. On the morning of that very day, as I took Judy a number of drafts, he said, in Miss Levey's hearing, "Are you doing anything to-night?"

"To-night? I'm afraid I am," I replied, though solely for Miss Levey's benefit. "To-morrow I'm not."

"To-morrow won't do. You're a dashed difficult man to get, Jeffries!"

"You should have given me a little notice," I said, though foreseeing already that Pepper would eat Miss Levey's supper that night.

"Well, we'll talk about it presently; if you can possibly put your engagement off, do.... Now, Miss Levey——"

He began to give instructions to Miss Levey.

Later in the morning Miss Levey sought me.

"Oh, Mr Jeffries," she began, very *empressée*, "I think we won't come to-night. Mr Pepper——"

"It is rather awkward," I admitted. "I'm awfully sorry——"

"Please don't apologise. It really doesn't matter. I can come up any evening, you know."

"Well, in that case——"

"We'll fix another evening. I know you and Mr Pepper have private affairs."

"Yes," I thought, not very graciously, "and to be in at 'em's the only thing you want more than to pry into my domestic ones." But aloud I said, "It's awfully good of you—do tell Mr Aschael how sorry I am."

So it was Judy Pepper, and not Miriam Levey and Aschael, who dined at Verandah Cottage that night.

Were it for no other reason than to let you know a little of these Schmerveloff neighbours of mine I should have to tell you of Judy's visit that evening. This sounds a little portentous, as if my tale were about to take a sensational turn, with bombs and secret agents in it. Be calm, it is not; I only mention these Schmerveloffs as standing, in a way, for certain forces of which Pepper and I intended to make use. A very few words will explain what I mean.

We are not social theorists, Pepper and I; we have to handle social problems practically, as they come; and so in the wider humanitarian sense we may be all wrong. But even then this Schmerveloff school of thought had its importance for us. It was very useful to us, for instance, when the Aliens' Act was drafting; and with the outbreak of Syndicalism, with all the bearings that has had on Trades Disputes, it became very important indeed. Perhaps, after all, the only hint I need give you as to the way in which we handled it is this: that, the rate of progress of this International Socialism being necessarily that of the slowest-moving and most backward partner in the alliance—Russia—we have used that fact either as a drag on Syndicalism or as an apparent encouragement of it, as the needs of the moment dictated. And when I say "apparent encouragement," I mean that we have winked at all this translation from the Russian pessimists that has harnessed art to purposes of social propaganda. That, since racial development is of far greater lasting weight than economic theory, has seemed to us the readiest way of letting folk see that Russia's problems are not necessarily ours; and if we can only keep Syndicalism in check, they may Russianise our literature completely for all Pepper and I care.

So we talked of Russia that night. Evie, as soon as she had seen Pepper instead of Miss Levey, had worked herself into a flurry in changing preparations at the last moment, and had had to run out for candles for our guest's candlesticks. But when dinner was at last served, half-an-hour late, nowhere could have been found a prettier waitress than we had—Evie herself. Indeed, she seemed to prefer waiting to dining. As long as she was doing things she felt herself on safe ground; it was the folding hands afterwards to talk to

The Debit Account

our terribly engaging visitor that she dreaded. She strove to attain by little formalisms what he achieved by the mere ease of nature, and, as she stuck tenaciously to it, I admired what was neither more nor less than a kind of courage in her. We finished dinner, and ascended to the drawing-room, I carrying those cumbersome candlesticks.

Pepper worked really hard that night to put Evie at her ease, but alas! through no fault of anybody's, but by the sheer decreeing of the stars, his labours were not a success. The first accident he had was when he asked her how she found her neighbours, compelling her to say that she didn't find them at all—didn't know them. And when he said, "Ah, Russians are like that," and related an anecdote, she perturbed me a little by asking him whether he had been in Russia—for I did not know that the extraordinary man had, and fancied the question not very kindly put. But Pepper surprised me by saying "Oh yes," and went on to tell more stories....

With these stories he was safe for a time, but presently he again had bad luck. He was speaking, as if he had come for no other purpose than to tell us travellers' tales, of the difficulty of the Russian language, which I gathered to be great; and suddenly he said, "But it's an exceedingly valuable asset from a commercial point of view. Should you have a boy to put into business, Mrs Jeffries, let him learn Russian."

It was, of course, hyper-sensitive of Evie, but not unnatural in the circumstances. She coloured deeply; she rose; she said good-night; and even then Pepper was not at the end of his troubles, for, advancing punctiliously to open the bedroom door for her, that insecure old door, that always opened at a touch, flew back, displaying the unmade bed on which Evie had lain that afternoon, and the general disorder of the interior. Pepper was already in the midst of a deep bow, but he must have seen.... After that I got him whisky; we settled down to our talk, and, ordinary speech being plainly audible from the bedroom, he dropped his voice to match my own tones—and was, I dare say, heartily glad when the evening was over.

This mention of our cramped quarters reminds me that I may as well get those inconveniences of which I told you over at once. To save time, I will tell you both what they were then, and what they afterwards became.

I had begun well-nigh to hate children. The schools, you see, had not yet reopened, and urchins played under our windows till half-past nine or ten o'clock at night. I frequently had work in the evenings that demanded close concentration, and it mostly happened that, when I sat down to it, as if by appointment the noise began. I do not know which howl or thump or bump was the most hideous. Iron hoops, driven with a hooked iron rod, were bad, but the shouts and whoops and calls, all in a blood-curdling Cockney accent, were worse; for while by great resolution you can nerve yourself to endure an iron hoop, you never know which yell or shout a child is going to emit next. These had all the horror of unexpectedness. I used to make mental bets on it, and I was always wrong.... And then sometimes there would come an endless racket that resembled nothing so much as a fire-engine in full career, which, on descending, I should discover to come from a diminutive cart at the end of a string, pulled by a toddler of four.

Sometimes these noises drove me half frantic. I carried my papers from the dining-room to the drawing-room—thence to the bedroom—I even tried the kitchen; and this, mark you, was important work, work that has since, I may say without boasting, become of national value. I spoke to policemen—I even used the power of beauty, and got Evie to speak to policemen—but only to be told that they were as helpless as I: "Children is eddicated now, and not as afraid of bobbies as they used to be." And on a fatal evening I was so unthinking as to distribute a number of pennies in order to buy an hour's peace for a calculation that seriously involved the interests of three shipping lines. That settled it. Thenceforward I was never without children. One Sunday afternoon I forgot myself and

The Debit Account

boxed the ears of the biggest of them. That brought round a parent—not a father, but a mother.... Ugh!——

And the house itself was far too small. Billy Izzard's sketches on our walls shook to my tread, and passing vans made the very foundations tremble. In order to get even our small belongings into the place Evie had to put boxes inside boxes, and boxes inside these again, so that in the finding of a garment she had not worn for some time the whole tiny bedroom floor was choked with boxes. Save for the little recess in the kitchen, the triangular cupboard under the stairs was the only storage accommodation we had. With the greatest care, Evie could not always avoid hanging an old skirt over my best hopsack (West's, Bond Street), or mislaying some article of which I had need in the very moment of bolting for my bus. And worst of all was that screen on the verandah that gave us nothing to look at but a short slope of parched green. Verandah Cottage! By Jove, yes!...

One other thing I will mention, though this did not come till the winter. The neighbouring house, which hitherto had been a tomb, became alive. I never knew the reason for this sudden awakening, nor whether Schmerveloff had suddenly found himself reduced to taking in lodgers, or whether he was merely holding out a helping hand to co-revolutionaries in the hour of their need; but I do know that presently he began to have a succession of extraordinary visitors. Hairy, uncouth-looking men, with soft hats, came for a week or a month, and brought their women, fat, spare, astrakhan-capped or bare-headed. They wore smocks and embroidered *portières*, and worked at peasant industries. One of them had a child, the sweetest of little girls—but oh, her sweetness vanished from me when she began to play at all hours in the garden, shouting, crowing, and impossible to turn away! I went so far as to wait on Schmerveloff himself about this dreadful child, and was told that, inconvenient as these things might be to me, the question was not a private one at all. It was a Social Question. Society oppressed them, they oppressed me; it was Society that was wrong.... I told our fellows this afterwards, when the Aliens' Act was drafting; Robson was immensely amused. "What did you say?" he asked.... Of course there was nothing to say....

And then, about Christmas, the Social Question became acute indeed. For the development of the peasant industries the most Asiatic barber-robber of the lot set up a furnace, a lathe and an anvil....

No wooden walls (save Nelson's) could have kept that racket out....

Had the sum of the world's beautiful things been added to, I could have grinned and borne it, but it was beaten copper-work the Asiatic made.

And I could do nothing.

I pass on.

Weeks before this invasion of beards and embroidered casement-cloth, I earnestly hoped that my firstborn, when I should have one, would never remember that little house with the glass-panelled door and the verandah. But the prospect of our "domestic event," as Miss Levey called it, hardly weighed on me yet. I gave little heed to Louie Causton's prophecy, that I might sooner or later find myself driven to take the desperate course of telling Evie what, so far, only Louie and myself knew; and I did not see, as Louie seemed to see, where the peril lay. If it was only a question of keeping Evie busy and amused for a little while longer, I thought I should be able to manage that. Only later did I see myself as a man who pours water constantly into a vessel and tells himself that because the level remains the same there is no leak. I still intended to stand between Evie and Life. In effect, if necessary, I would live much of her life for her. And now let me, before I leave this part of my tale, tell you briefly what that life was at its loveliest.

V

Had there ever been any shadow of a division between Evie and myself, which there had not, it must have vanished now. I did not attempt to conceal from myself that her gifts did not extend in all directions equally. Socially expert in Pepper's sense, for example, she could hardly yet be expected to be, and I should have been unreasonable to have reproached her for not grasping the intricate problems that, if the truth must be told, frequently filled Pepper and myself with perplexity. But these things are independent of deep humanity, and by as much as she fell short in them she was richly dowered in other ways. It was still the love of a woman I wanted, not the semblance of a masculine friendship; and I had it, and was glad at the thought of my rich possession. Often, for pure emotion, I caught her in my arms when I saw her, rejoicing yet timorous before that which was presently to come to pass; and whether it was a pallor that sometimes crossed her face, or a sudden glow as of some warm and Venetian underpainting or else a smiling, happy lassitude infinitely moving in its appeal, all spoke of the pledge that had been given and taken between us.

Quite past telling was the peace this pledge brought to me. I was, after all, to begin anew. Despite Life's mauling of my hapless self, here was a tiny white leaf preparing for the writing of a record that should supersede and obliterate my own. Deeper things than men know were seeing to that ushering, and by nothing less miraculous than a birth was I going to be delivered from the body of that haggard death. Often, as I seemed to be busily writing at our small folding table, I quite lost myself in the contemplation of this coming manumission; and day by day, looking out over Waterloo Place and the Mall, I conjured up her image—resting while Aunt Angela (who now came up from Woburn Place almost daily) dusted or swept or washed up, taking her easy walks on the Heath, sewing (though not now for herself), or doing such light work as would not tire her. Fortunately, the Social Question next door had reached the crisis of over-production in the beaten-copper market; a glut had supervened; and the making of the wooden bowls and carved porridge-sticks that are designed for oppressed serfs and sold at a high price to the amateurs of the Difficult Life, caused less disturbance to our panels and pictures. The whooping child too had gone.

Aunt Angela had bought Evie a deep wicker basket lined with pale blue, and with the greatest circumspection I delayed to fill this basket too quickly. We talked for a week before making a purchase, and, in one case, for quite three weeks. This was when I bought, at a shop near Great Turnstile, what Evie called a "jangle"—a beautiful Jacobean coral mounted in silver, with many silver bells and a faint piping whistle at one end. Both as I entered the shop and left it again a grey nightmare tried to fasten itself upon me, of a woman who had forgotten where she lived, walking the Fields round the corner, alone at night; but I shook the horror off.... Even down to such details did I keep Evie from fancies—for she had fancies, the ousting of which was a matter for diversion rather than argument. One of these fancies was that she now wanted to see Miriam Levey. Another was that she did not want, just then at any rate, to see Louie Causton.

For as it chanced, Louie came the nearest (though with a nearness sad enough) to a married woman of anybody she happened at present to know; this, of course, largely as a result of my own exclusive attitude. Aunt Angela, by virtue of George and her other experiences, knew as much as ten married women, and that was frequently precisely the difficulty. Certain charwomen, I gathered, inured to immoderate families, gave Evie the benefit of their advice now and then, but that was about all. And it was one evening as I cast about for an opening to introduce Louie's name that Evie herself said once more that she would like to see Miss Levey.

"Certainly," I said, with a readiness that was only the result of seeing no way out of it this time. "As long as she won't tire you."

"I won't let her do that," Evie promised.

"All right," I said.... "And by the way"—I put this as if it had just occurred to me—"should you care to have Louie Causton up if Billy knows where to find her?"

"Yes, I should some time—but not just now, dear. You'll tell Miriam, then?"

"Yes."

I had promised it before I remembered something that might have made me less ready to promise it. It was now the beginning of October. We had to take our holidays in rotation at the F.B.C.; for a fortnight I had been working late in order that Whitlock might take his; and next on the list in our department was Miss Levey. Grumbling that it was almost too late to take a holiday at all, she was going away for a week-end only. Instantly, I saw what that meant....

The next day I capitulated to her as gracefully as I could.

"You'll be able to have a really satisfactory visit now, a whole day," I said. "It would only have been a couple of hours before."

"I'll take *such* good care of her!" she purred.

"I am sure you will," I said conciliatingly....

Three days later Miss Levey was up at Verandah Cottage. She was up there the next day also. Although she had always gone by the time I returned at night, she was up several times after that.

Well, it couldn't be helped ... and I was going to tell you, not about Miriam Levey, but about my happiness and Evie's.

Today, in my house in Iddesleigh Gate, there are many things thrust into dark corners that will ever occupy odd corners of my heart. They are the pieces of furniture from that poky old place in the Vale of Health. The people of my household tell me they are shabby, but as I never see them divorced from a hundred gentle associations, their shabbiness matters nothing to me. In the children's day-nursery there is the old shop-damaged couch from the Tottenham Court Road cellar. Its pegamoid is frayed and its springs broken, but Evie lay on it before those destructive little hands came into being. She lay on it with her legs wrapped in an old, faded, mignonette-coloured Paisley shawl—for presently the days were shortening, we had started fires, and Verandah Cottage was a Cave of the Winds for draughts; and my housekeeper had a bad five minutes only the other day when that shawl nearly went out of the house with the bottles and crates and old rags. The bookshelves Evie used to dust and polish still serve me; and quite a number of smaller things, including that first wicker basket into which the "jangle" was put (Evie keeps that) carry my mind back in a twinkling to that early time.

Evie had her little jokes about our unborn mite. Still further to repair the slight on Hampton Court of our Greenwich honeymoon, the infant at one time was to be called "Hampton," but as she had ten different names for it each week, a name more or less didn't matter. Its eyes were to be so-and-so—the colour also varied day by day. If a boy, it was to be of my own bone and stature; if a girl, less. I used to joke with her when, seeing her brooding and gently smiling, I pretended to discover these and a hundred other patterns and specifications in her eyes; but, however lovely these imaginings were, they were no lovelier than herself. Though the days now seemed less long, the little *élans* with which she ran to me when she heard my step at night were a passionate rendering of herself far greater than before; and I will end this part of my tale with the first time, the very first, I heard her sing.

She had gone into the bedroom that night, and I had heard her moving about; and then there had stolen out low contralto notes that might have belonged to somebody else, so new were they to me.... She was happy. She was so happy that she was learning to sing. I stood listening, with tears gathering in my eyes and suddenly rolling down my cheeks....

She was happy....

She did not know why, a few moments later, with the face of one who hears joyful news, I pushed at the bedroom door and took her, half ready for bed as she was, into my arms.

Oh, to hear her, of her own accord, sing—and to know that soon her song would not more gently rock those feeble limbs and close those unknowing eyes than it now brought rest to my own weary frame and sleep to my own heavy eyes, weary with watching for the day that at last, at last was coming!

PART III WELL WALK

I

As far as my worldly position is concerned, two leaps have sufficed to place me where I stand to-day—the first from the Vale of Health to the Well Walk, not a quarter of a mile away, and the second from Well Walk to Iddesleigh Gate. I am omitting such interludes as furnished rooms for short periods and odd times in which I have packed Evie off with the children to the seaside. We were in the Vale of Health for exactly a year, and in Well Walk for three. I took the Iddesleigh Gate House, wonderful ceilings and Amaranth Room and all, from the late Baron Stillhausen.

But this is a very summary statement of what my real advance has been. Those who have called me a lucky man—which on the whole I also am persuaded I am—know nothing of my hidden labour. Of this, since it is just beginning to show in the contemporary history of my country, I cannot say very much; and so, picking out a fact here and an incident there, I shall take leave for the rest of my tale to keep as closely as may be to my increasingly intricate personal story.

The incident with which I will resume—the incident which resulted in Louie Causton's appointment to the post still held by Miss Levey—came about as follows.

In taking the Well Walk house—(here I am skipping six months; my infant son was born; I still had seven or eight weeks to run with the F.B.C., but already our plans were perfected, and the new Consolidation had already secured its premises in Pall Mall)—in taking the Well Walk house I had made a woeful miscalculation of how far the Verandah Cottage furniture would go. Indeed I had so over-estimated its quantity that our new abode was almost as bare as a barracks, and, occupied as I was with important business, I had almost got used to its barrenness. But as Evie had to live in the place, I had found that I really must raise a sum of money for carpets, curtains, and other things indispensable to married folk who find themselves three; and I had decided that part of the one hundred pounds I got as an advance from Pepper was going to be spent on a dining-room table that I had not always to remember I must not sit down on. Well, on a Saturday afternoon in October this table came. I saw it into the dining-room, and then, feeling the need of air, I put on my hat and coat and took a walk as far as the Whitestone Pond. There I met Billy Izzard, in the dickens of a temper.

"Well, how goes it, Billy?" I asked cheerfully, seeing that he was put out. Billy's grumblings always have the effect of cheering me up.

He looked up, scowled, and then resumed his gazing across the Pond. Then he watched the passage of a horse and cart through the water, looked up again, and broke out.

"It goes rottenly—that's how it goes!" he growled. "Do you remember coming into my place one evening when I had a girl sitting for me—tallish girl, with a perfectly exquisite figure—Louie Causton her name was?"

I said that I did remember it.

"Well, she's the trouble. I want her—must have her—and I can't get her. She says she isn't sitting any more; her doctor's forbidden it. Her doctor!... The jade's as sound as a bell; she never had a doctor in her life, I'll swear; she just won't sit, doesn't want to. She wheedled that sketch out of me too, the one I was doing that day—walked off with it under her arm—stole it, practically—and now I can't get her for love or money."

This interested me. It interested me so much that to conceal my interest, I made a joke. "Oh? Tried both?" I said; but Billy went on.

"Perhaps she'll change her mind when she finds she's nothing to live on. She'll sit in costume, it appears; some cock and bull story about chills; and she said, Couldn't I paint her in some old supers' duds that she can hire at the Models' Club for sixpence a day?—me painting theatrical wardrobes *à la* Coleman, Roma?... And her crochet!"

"What about her crochet?"

"Her crochet? Why, when I told her she wouldn't make fifteen shillings a week as Marguerite with the jewel-casket—she's not pretty—I told her so—she said she could fall back on her crochet! A goddess, I tell you ... and she pitches me a tale about a doctor that she can't help laughing at herself!"

He ran on, to Louie's detriment from his special point of view, but already I was wondering what her own point of view might be.

That I had not heard from Louie since that night of the Berkeley dinner had been, as far as it went, reassuring. Had she needed me, or I her, whichever in the tangled circumstances it might be, I should have heard from her; and I had had no reason for seeking her out. When Evie had told me that Louie now had charge of Kitty Windus she had told me nothing that I had not already known; and as Evie had had this from Miriam Levey, I find I must break off for a moment to speak of my relation with that lady.

Since she had got her fat, high-heeled foot inside my door, Miss Levey's devotion to Evie had been as unremitting as if, lacking her attentions, my little son would never have got himself born at all. Not a week had passed but she had dropped in once or twice, mostly alone, but not infrequently with the ringleted Aschael. It annoyed me that Evie should like her as much as apparently she did, and my annoyance was the greater that I could give no reason for it. One night I had given way rather petulantly to this annoyance.

The Debit Account

It had been just before we had left Verandah Cottage. Billy Izzard had come in and had made some remark about our Arab horsemen, and, more that I might relish its artistic vulgarity than for any other reason, I had taken one of these objects down from the mantelpiece. I had not known that I had held the thing in a rather vindictive grip until suddenly the plaster had broken in my hand. My other hand had made an instinctive movement by no means prompted by presence of mind. I had saved the body of the ornament from total smash, but the heads both of tamer and steed were in fragments. I had been on the point of throwing the ridiculous thing away, but had changed my mind, and put it back on the mantelpiece. Later I had expressed bland sorrow to Miss Levey, and had assured her that I was going to have it mended; but I had not done so during the remainder of our stay at Verandah Cottage. I did not know what had become either of it or of its companion statue.

During the last anxious days before the birth of our child, Miss Levey had triumphed over me completely. There had been no withstanding her. She had bidden me fetch hot-water bottles, had informed me when it was time for Evie to go to bed, and, conspiring with Aunt Angela, had, in a word, taken things out of my hands entirely. Once or twice she had overdone this even in Evie's eyes, but I had been dull enough not to see at first that her ascendancy over Evie was not direct, but mediate. Only lately had I discovered that Evie's real interest was, not in Miriam Levey, but in Kitty Windus.

For those talks I had dreaded yet had been powerless to prevent had already borne fruit. I don't think it was so much that Evie experienced again those compassions and magnanimities that had given her that gentle heartache in the tea-gardens on that Bank Holiday evening, as that she remembered the wish into which they had solidified—the wish to have Kitty completely off her mind. Miss Levey, I was pretty sure, had seen to it that this wish should become firmly fixed. She had evidently assumed, for example, that I should be adverse to a meeting between Kitty and Evie. "Your husband wouldn't like it," I could imagine her as having said; "quite naturally, my dear; one can't blame him; and so I suppose that ends it." And to the last words I could imagine her as having given the meaning, "We do seem to be dependent on the will of this dull opinionative sex for some reason or other—why I can't make out." Miss Levey, you see, was an economically emancipated woman.

So, though not a word had been said, Kitty had come, by reason of I knew not what sympathy Miriam Levey had worked up on her behalf, to be between Evie and myself. That poor Kitty deserved all the sympathy we could give her I had never a doubt, but you see the two things that stood in the way—the lesser thing that Miss Levey assumed I "should not like," and that other huge and fatal thing that was the truth. To the multitudinous harassings of my business these two things made a dense background of private harassings.... But I did not intend that another long and dogged duel should begin between Miriam Levey and myself. She was not going to be taken over by Pepper, Jeffries and the Consolidation. If this enterprise did anything at all it would do something very big indeed; soon I should be placed high above the wretched little Jewess's power to hurt; and after all, there is no man who attains to great power but leaves in his train a score of these carpers, wishful yet impotent to harm.

But the offering of the new post to Louie Causton was another matter. I hesitated and wavered. Plainly, I doubted whether I had the right to find Louie a job. In the close-packed fulness of her life, struggles and anxieties and all, her happiness consisted; and though she might need the money, as matters stood she had a peace that money could not give, and might take away. Let her, I thought at first, toil and keep her heaven.

But that, I thought presently, might be all very high and fine, but practically not very much to the point. Billy had been perfectly right when he had said that by costume-sitting and crochet she would hardly make fifteen shillings a week. I knew of old what heaven in

The Debit Account

those circumstances meant, and I had had no boy to look after, and no woman intermittently infirm. One can have too much even of heaven on those terms....

And yet it would be impossible to attach her to my own office. What I had seen in those grey eyes on the night of the Berkeley dinner would not brook daily meetings, dictation of letters, and the other duties I had already cast Whitlock for. Myself left out of the question, she, I was quite sure, would never accept it. Turn her over to Pepper, then? That would hardly be fair to Pepper, who might wish to choose for himself....

And one other thing, of which I will speak presently, had already caused my cheeks to burn.

Well, I should have to see what I could do.

It did not surprise me much that when I reached Well Walk again, Miss Levey was there. That echoing, half-furnished house of ours, I ought to say, was on the south side of the Walk, and my own study was on the ground floor at the back, with Evie's drawing-room immediately overhead. I heard this drawing-room door open as I entered, and it was on the bare half-landing, against the red and blue window, with cut-glass stars round its border, that I saw Miss Levey's flamingo-coloured costume with the black satin buttons.

"Oh, here he is," Evie was saying; "he'll take you on to your bus. Good-bye, Miriam, dear—remember me to Aschael——"

"Good-bye, darling—don't forget, will you?"

"Good-bye."

I remember that it was as I took Miss Levey to her bus that afternoon that she asked me to call her by her Christian name. Instantly I did so—and forgot her request again with a promptitude even greater. To tell the truth, that "Remember me to Aschael" of Evie's stuck a little in my throat. A little more ceremony, it seemed to me, would have fitted the relation better, and I differed from Miss Levey if she thought that in asking me to call her "Miriam," she, and not I, was conferring the favour. Therefore as I saw her off I again addressed her as "Miss Levey" and let her take it as an inadvertence or not as she list. Then, with that "Remember me to Aschael" again uppermost in my mind, I returned to Evie.

In hoping to see her alone, however, I was again disappointed. This time Aunt Angela was there. She was standing by the new dining-table, and apparently deploring my purchase.

"*What* a pity!" she was saying. "Just when I'd arranged for you to have that one of mine! I meant it as a surprise—oh, why didn't I tell you sooner!"

I have referred, I hope not unkindly, to a certain laxity in this dear and harmless spinster's hold on life. Since the birth of our child this laxity had become intensified, if such a word can be used of laxity, and very rarely had she come up to see us empty-handed. From some mysterious hoard of belongings that seemed ever on the point of exhaustion and yet ever stood the strain of another gift, she had brought, now a tiny pair of knitted woollen socks, now a shawl, now a bit of silver, and even the mite's cradle was that in which Evie herself had been rocked. She found a pleasure quite paradisal in these continual givings. I think they were her spiritual boasts of how little she required for herself.

"*What* a pity!" she purred again. "But I dare say they'd take it back——"

"Hallo!" I said, shaking hands. "Take what back? What's that you're saying?"

"This table. I'm sure they'd let you off your bargain for ten shillings or so. The money would be so much more useful."

I laughed. "Oh, money's no object," I said.

This, of course, was mere mischief. The truth was that Angela Soames, like Evie, had begun to hold my ambition a good deal in dread. It had been good fun to think about in the early stages; they had enjoyed that part as much as anybody; but to take the plunge as I was taking it was—in Miss Angela's case I might almost say "impious"; certainly it was a storming of destiny that was bound to bring a crop of consequences they were sure I had not sufficiently weighed. So it had become my habit to hold their timidity over them as a joke, talking sometimes in sums that might have staggered even the Consolidation. "Oh, money's no object!" I said, laughing.

"Well!" Aunt Angela retorted, "even you can't afford to throw it away till you've got it. So, Evie, I thought my round table in place of this one—send this back—and the tea-urn I promised you in the middle of the sideboard, with Mr. Pepper's candlesticks on each side of it—just here—and you could buy a quite nice pair of curtains with the pound Jeff turns up his nose at."

I interrupted. "Your tea-urn? Oh, come, come! We're not going to accept that!"

But she only dropped her eyes. "My wants are few," she said, "and I've more than enough for them. You young people come first. How do you know I haven't had a legacy?... And of course I shall have the table repolished, Evie, and if Jeff *will* be stupid, you can have it in the drawing-room, in that corner by the bureau——"

I was about to laugh again at the artless mixture in her of expansive unworldliness and quite astute machination when suddenly I thought better of it, and turned away. Aunt Angela was taking off her hat and giving coquettish touches to her tall, snowy hair. As that meant that she proposed to spend the evening with us, I had to postpone what I wished to say to Evie until she should have departed.

II

This was no more than that I thought the Christian name business was being a little overdone; but the more I thought of it, the less easy did it become to put. Perhaps you see my difficulty. It was, in a word, this: that a man on whom circumstances have pressed with such unique urgency that he has had, or conceived himself to have, no choice but to effect the removal of a fellow-being from the world, cannot take even so small a matter as this precisely as another man can. The quick of his soul is perpetually exposed. There are no trifles in his world. What is another man's slight annoyance is to him the menace of an assassination; another's nothings are his doom. A single unconscious touch and the toucher starts back with an amazed "What's this?"

Yet I have said that it was not remorse that bred this sensitiveness in me, and I hasten to maintain that. Remorse is a damage, in which a man is penally mulcted; but this of mine was no more than a price, fairly and squarely agreed upon, which I was prepared to pay. It was a heavy one; you may take my word for it that there is no more costly purchase in the whole market of human happenings than a righteous murder; but it still remained a price, in the fixing of which I had concurred. More than this: men have been known, from remorse, to give themselves up; but at the thought of such a surrender I grew hot and vehement. I appreciated the point of view of the very revolutionaries against whom my life's work has been directed. What! Suffer an outside judgment when I was acquitted in my own!... I laughed, and in my laughter found courage. Not I!...

The Debit Account

And a man is not in the grip of remorse who, asked whether he would do his deed again, can reply with a deep "By heaven—yes!"

Nevertheless, I was perilously open. I alone among men could not rebuff the freedom of a Christian name without bringing my soul into the transaction; nay, I could not even buy a dining-table without having (as I had just had) to check an utterance and to turn away. For at Aunt Angela's words, "How do you know I haven't had a legacy?" I had become vigilant again. She had had no legacy; I knew that; but she *had* been twice or thrice to Guildford, and, if she wished to indulge herself in the luxury of giving, would be likely to make the most rather than the least of whatever mementoes of the late Mrs Merridew she might have chanced to come by. You see how, on an afternoon taken at random, two nothings had made still denser by a fraction that background of which I was every moment conscious. I was beginning to realise that I was the man who was denied the luxury of carelessness. I might not jest or laugh or move a finger without first looking around the corner. I went hampered among free men. I tell you it is a hard thing to live in a world that has no trifles....

Still, exposed or guarded, I had my life to live, and I was no longer disposed in the matter of this intimacy with Miss Levey to do nothing at all. Therefore, when I returned from seeing Aunt Angela away and found Evie still in the dining-room, I took my risk.

She ought to have been in bed; but instead she had drawn up a chair to an old bureau, and was quite unnecessarily fiddling with old papers and letters and nondescript objects put away in the nest of drawers. She looked up as I entered, and the vivacity with which she spoke seemed a little forced.

"Fancy, Jeff!" she exclaimed, her fingers in the leaves of some old twopenny notebook or other, "I can actually read my old shorthand yet! I should have thought I'd forgotten all about it, after all this time! I'll bet I could read as quickly as you!"

I stirred the dying fire. "Isn't it time you were in bed?" I said.

"Oh, just let me tidy this—I sha'n't be many minutes."

And while I picked up an evening paper she went on with her pottering about the bureau.

But the light sound of the moving paper began to get a little on my nerves. It does that sometimes. I suppose it's like some people fidgeting if there is a cat in the room. And presently I noticed that when she supposed me to be busily reading the rustling stopped. It was no good going on like this; the sooner I came to the point and said what I had to say, the better. I thought for a moment, and then put down my newspaper.

"Evie——" I said.

"Yes, dear?" she said brightly....

I put it with perfect gentleness. Suddenness and sharpness also are among the trifles of life I had had to forego. When I had finished, she did not seem surprised. She only nodded once or twice.

"I see," she said slowly. "Well, Miriam—I mean Miss Levey, if you wish it, dear——"

"No, darling; I don't know that I go as far as that. I was only speaking of these broadcast intimacies."

"Miriam, then—Miriam said you would object——"

"Well, I never denied Miriam a certain acuteness."

But she shook her head. For a minute or two I had been sure that I was not the only one who had something to say. When she did go on, it was at first haltingly, and then with just such a little setting of her resolution as she had used when, years ago, a sweet and awkward flapper, she had complimented me on my spurious engagement to the lady whose name she now suddenly mentioned.

"I don't mean to object to—to what you've been saying, Jeff. I mean—I mean object to this about poor Kitty. I know," she quickened, as if to forestall a remark, "that we haven't said anything about it—you and I—for a long time—but"—once more the rush—"I've felt you've known what I've been thinking, Jeff——"

I gained a little time. "But I wasn't speaking of Kitty Windus, dear," I said. "It was something quite different."

Then, before her look of trouble and appeal, I ceased my pretence.

"Very well, dearest," I sighed. "But tell me one thing. If I hadn't said anything to-night, *you* wanted to say something."

"Yes," she mumbled in a low voice to the twopenny notebook.

"Is that what Miss Levey meant when she said 'Don't forget' an hour or two ago?"

"Yes."

"You hadn't to forget to—to bring something, whatever it is, up about Kitty?"

Her silence told me that that was so. Then, slowly:

"And why should she think I should object to that?" I asked.

Evie's manner changed with almost electrical suddenness. She thrust her hands into her lap, straightened her back, and spoke almost victoriously.

"*There!* I *knew*! I told her so!" she triumphed. "'Miriam,' I said, 'you're *quite* wrong in thinking that—that——'"

"In thinking there's something to be ashamed of in an old engagement you've changed your mind about?" I suggested gently.

"Yes!" she exulted. "I said to her, 'Jeff wouldn't in the *least* mind my going to see her if I wanted'—and you wouldn't, would you, Jeff?"

"No," I said quickly. I said it quickly lest I should not say it at all. Then I qualified. "No.... One shrinks from pain, that's all, either enduring it or giving it."

"Giving Kitty pain?"

"Well, does Miss Levey think it would be pleasant to her—or is she merely willing to hurt her if she can hurt me too?"

"But—but—Miriam says she would really be awfully pleased—Kitty would—and I'm sure you're wrong, Jeff, about things like that lasting for years and years! They don't. I——" She checked herself.

But whether it was the check or what not that made the difference, all at once she started forward from the bureau and sank on her knees at my side. She herself put one of my hands about her waist, as if to compel it to a caress, and stroked her cheek against the other. The words she murmured were disjointed enough, but her tone was, oh, so eloquent....

"Dear, dear!" she besought me. "Miriam *was* wrong, wasn't she? Not that I care in the very least, only I've been, oh, so wretched, thinking there was something between us! I don't want to see her—Miriam—nor Kitty—very much—but it was so lonely—till Jack came—and there isn't anything now, is there, Jeff? I know there has been—but it's gone now, hasn't it?... Great strong hand!" She moistened it with her breathing.... "But it *is* all right now, isn't it, Jeff?"

I did not know why, all in a moment, I found myself remembering that curious prophecy of Louie Causton's: "I think you'll find that sooner or later you've got to tell her." Perhaps it was that in that moment I had my first glimpse of what Louie had really meant. Already it was useless to say there had been no slight shadow between us; Evie, who knew few things, at least knew that; but I had not dared to acknowledge it for fear of worse.... Yes, I began to see; and with my seeing I again grew hot and rebellious.

The Debit Account

Why, since the act I had committed had had at least as much of good as of evil in it, should I be hounded thus? Why should trifles accrete to an ancient and hideous memory until it became a corporeal, living, malignant thing? Why should that commonest of experiences, an old rescinded engagement, not, in my case also, be what Evie thought it was—a wound made whole again, or at any rate so hardened over that it could be touched without provoking a sharp scream of pain? It was intolerable....

Oh, never, if you can help it, live in a world without trifles!

Evie, at my knee, continued to supplicate. "Oh, darling, I've so, *so* wanted it to be like it was at first! Do you remember—in Kensington Gardens, sweetheart?"

And she turned up those loveliest eyes I ever looked into....

It had been in Kensington Gardens, early on a September evening, that I had asked her to marry me. Our chairs had been so drawn back into the clump of laurels that the man with the tickets had not noticed us, and we ourselves had seen little but a distant corner of the Palace, and, forty yards away across the grass, a dead ash gilded by the setting sun. At the F.B.C. Pepper had just begun to single out his new Jun. Ex. Con. for special jobs, and as a matter of fact I had had a small rise of salary that very week. Little enough it had been; certainly not enough to warrant me in exchanging our footing—one of increasingly frequent calls at Woburn Place and goodness knows how much lingering in likely streets on the chance of a sight of her—for a more explicit relation; but—well, as I say, I had thrust all else recklessly aside, and that evening had asked her to marry me.

There are some things that one must needs exaggerate if one is to speak of them at all; so if I say that at first it had seemed to her that my proposal was merely that two bruised spirits should thenceforward make the best of things together, I must leave you to discount that. I don't think she had known clearly what she had felt. The hand I had taken had trembled a little, and in the great dark eyes that had looked steadfastly away to the dead ash I had fancied I had discerned the beginnings of a refusal—a refusal out of mere customariness and a settled acceptance of our former relation. I had fancied that——

But even to the trembler a tremble may speak truer than words, and she had trembled and become conscious of it. For the first time it had occurred to her, sweet soul, that we had been all unconsciously passing from friendship to love, and were now making the discovery together. She had not known that I had never had anything but love from which to pass; and another access of trembling had taken her....

"The last evening you and I had a walk together," she had whispered at last, her eyes still gravely on the pale ash, "we—we didn't think of—this."

(Did I mention that during all the time I had known her we had only spent one other evening out of doors alone together? It had been more than four years before, and we had heard a nightingale sing on Wimbledon Common.)

I had not answered. To allow the memory of that other evening to repossess her had seemed the best answer to make. For though we pack our hearts daily with the stuff of life, only time shows us which is the tinsel we have coveted, and which the lump we have not known to be gold. More than four years had passed; presently those four years would have opened her eyes to differences too; and so I had waited....

And, if not yet discovered, at any rate sudden and troubling new questions had crowded into her eyes as I had watched. Another silence of many minutes, then:

"We've been such friends up to now," she had faltered, as much to the darkening evening as to myself.

"Need that mean 'No,' Evie?"...

"I don't know—it's so—strange—I never——"

I had drawn a little nearer.

"Never? Never once? You never once thought that perhaps——?"

Then once more had come the memories of that other evening, with the unhappiness of another's bringing, and the comfort of my own. Night had begun to creep under the trees, but the shadows but made zenith the purer. On such evenings lovers vie with one another in looking for the first star, but we were not lovers yet, and could see nothing save the ash, now become grey, and away to the north the faint yellow haze of the Bayswater Road. Evie's own figure had become dim until little of it had showed but the handkerchief in her lap, the narrow white stripe of her black and white blouse where her little black jacket parted, and, as at last she had turned, the motion of her eyes.

"You don't want an answer now, Jeff," she had said quickly, immediately dropping the eyes again.

But I had wanted my answer there and then.

"Now," I had replied as quickly as she, with I know not what grimness and resolution mingled with my tenderness.

"Not now, Jeff—I'm fonder of you than of anybody—you know that—but—but——"

But if her "buts" had included the vanished Kitty Windus, Archie Merridew, or anything else from that four-year-old dustheap, I had allowed them to avail her little. Over my heart too had come that nightingale's song, heard by a still mere, and her hapless sobbing on my breast because Life was harsh, and my own desperate struggle not to clasp her there and then. Repression so powerful as that had been is not given twice to a man, at any rate not to such a man as I; nor had I thought that she, whose tremors were more eloquent than her speech, had desired it either.... "Not now, Jeff—please—soon——" she had half sobbed, shrinking as it were from the wonder of her own enlightenment; and her handkerchief had fallen to the grass....

The next moment, in returning it to her, I had had her in my arms.

Those truer tidings than any words of hers could give expression to had come from the lips that had not even sought to avoid mine. Sought to avoid them? I call the first star that peeped through the laurels to witness the handful of dust that friendship of ours had become. Speech? Language? She used neither; to me in that moment she *was* both speech and language—vocal flesh, her very hair and eyes an utterance. You will not ask me an utterance of what; I take my chance of being understood in the light of what Woman is to you. Make her what you will: a riddle herself—or the answer to the deepest enigma of the soul; as much earth as a man's hard hands must needs be filled with—or as much spirit as he can bear until he himself is all spirit; a lovely casket—yet not too lovely for the scroll of the Freedom it contains. Have it your own way. I only know that if she spoke thus I heard as if my whole body had been one attuned and exquisite nerve. We had drawn a little deeper into the laurels.... Again we kissed....

And in my heart there had been jealousy of no man, dead or living. That dead young man had awakened her from sleep, but I had made her mine with her eyes wide open. He had taken her by surprise, but me she had chosen. And as our lips had met once more, I had known that she loved even the pain I caused her in straining her in my arms.

"You never once—never once thought of it?" I had said huskily at last.

"Dear—dear! How *was* I to?"

"Kiss me—kiss me——"

And now, on her knees at my knee by our dying dining-room fire, she asked me if I remembered that evening in Kensington Gardens.

All at once I vowed that I wouldn't stand it—wouldn't stand the intervention of anything on earth, whether of my own making or another's, between us and that first joy. And again, as I held her, I thought of Louie's words. Louie was right—or at least half right. For the present the shadow had passed, but unless I did something now, it would return. Again we should drift apart, and Miss Levey would keep us so. If I did not partly explain, circumstances might do so entirely. Yes, Louie was so far right. If I was to keep the dearest thing on earth to me, I must make a half-truth seem to guarantee the false remainder, and tell Evie of that cruel Kitty Windus episode.

And so I come to my first, though not to my last, attempt to tell without telling, and, as they say, to make my omelette without breaking my eggs.

Her cheek was still against my hand; I looked mournfully down on her. With such a goal it didn't much matter where I began.

"What do you suppose, darling," I began, "Miss Levey's object is in all this?"

Evie's eyes moved to the mantelpiece. It was a bare entablature of black marble, with nothing on it but a small Swiss clock and one or two cabinet photographs—no Arab horsemen. Shyly she glanced from the mantelpiece corner, where the horsemen should have been, to me.

"Yes, she asked to-day whether you'd got it mended," she murmured.

"Do you really like her?"

"I was so lonely, Jeff," she pleaded.

"Poor child!... Evie——"

She looked quickly up at my change of tone.

"What?"

"I want to tell you what her object is. I don't find it easy."

"What do you mean, Jeff?" she asked, strangely abruptly.

"And I'm afraid you won't find it easy either."

She had dropped my hand. "Jeff, what do you mean?"

"I mean that she thinks she's found out—is finding out—something discreditable about me."

At first I did not understand the change, almost to horror, that came into Evie's eyes. Only after a moment almost of fear of what I saw there did I fathom her thought. I don't know how men speak who have an unfaithfulness to confess to their wives, but it flashed on me that Evie actually thought it might be that—so can pure innocence and worldly experience be pierced by the same fear.

"Jeff," she said faintly, her colour all gone, "don't you—haven't you—loved me?"

"Loved you?" I laughed for the irony of it. "Yes, dearest," I said quietly, "I've loved you. Never fear for that. That was the beginning of it all."

"The beginning?"

"Of what Miss Levey thinks. Dear, could you bear to think she's right, and that I've been a blackguard?"

So great was her suspense that the little sound she made was one almost of irritation. "Oh, Jeff, say what you've got to say——"

"It's why I spoke of causing pain to Kitty Windus——"

"Oh, you're cruel——!"

I moistened my lips. "Very well...."

The Debit Account

Locked up in my private desk, written in Pitman's shorthand, there lies a full statement of that curious affair of mine with Kitty Windus; but I am not going to quote from that statement here. So long as it is understood that that heartless thing had existed side by side with a love for Evie that had never for a moment wavered, that is all that matters. I had now no longer a thought for the undesirableness, the danger even, of a meeting between Evie and Kitty; risky though that would be, I now saw nothing save that we were reunited, and that we could only remain so by passing on to her a portion of my shame. If you don't see this you are lucky. Your life has trifles in it. You can buy dining-tables, and use or reject the familiarity of Christian names. You have not had to carry upon your shoulders a weight greater than a man can support, nor to choose which portion you are to leave on the road behind you unless your back is to break. You have not known the conclusion to which—but you shall hear the conclusion to which I have been driven all in good time.

In the meantime, sparing myself in her eyes no more than I am sparing myself in yours now, I told her how little she had ever had to fear from Kitty Windus.

The hands of the tiny Swiss clock on the mantelpiece pointed to half-past ten by the time I had finished. I gazed at the clock dully, thinking for a moment how little time my recital had occupied. Then I remembered that the hands had pointed to half-past ten before I had begun.... Mechanically I took the clock down and wound it up. To wind up a clock was something to do until Evie should speak.

She had not once interrupted me. At one point of my story she had merely got up from my knee and seated herself in a low rocking-chair, in which she now rocked softly. As I still sat with the clock in my hands I tried idly to remember at which point of my story she had got up; it might be an indication of her state of mind; but I forgot this again, and found myself examining the back of the clock almost with curiosity. I did not look at her. I put the clock back on the mantelpiece again and once more sat down, still without looking at her. Glancing presently at the clock again I saw that its hands pointed to five and twenty minutes to eleven. I had wound it up, but had forgotten to set it right. That again was something to do. I adjusted it by my watch, and again sat down.

Then she spoke, and my heart sank. There was nothing in her tone but wonderment—wonderment, not at the story I had told her, but that I should have found it worth telling at all.

After all that portentous preparation—only that!

Odd enough, of course—sad enough, if you liked—but——

"Well, but, Jeff," she said, puzzled, "what about it?"

"Don't you see?" I asked, in a lower voice.

"Of course I see—how do you mean, 'see'? And I think you were awfully stupid. She was *bound* to find out, and she did find out, and left you, poor dear. It was absurd from beginning to end. Really I shall begin to think myself clever and you a simpleton, if that's all you've been moping about."

As you see, I had not advanced matters by one single inch.

"It *is* all, isn't it, Jeff?" she asked anxiously, suddenly sitting forward in the rocking-chair. "I don't mean," she went on more anxiously still, "that the whole thing wasn't awfully queer—not quite nice, dear, to speak the truth—but—but"—again there returned that quick look of fear with which she had asked me whether I had not loved her—"but—there wasn't—anything—Jeff?"

I sank back in my chair.

"No, there wasn't—anything," I said wearily.

"Then, Jeff——" she cried gladly.

And the next moment she was at my knee again, overflowing with comfort and compassion.

"You poor boy—you poor darling boy!" she crooned, so melted by my contrition that my offence went uncondemned. "Poor love!... And," she looked adorably up, "how *could* Evie reproach you, Jeff, when it was all for her? Darling!" she broke out, "*you* ought to reproach *me*, for thinking.... But you were so fearfully solemn.... I thought perhaps you hadn't loved Evie.... *Has* always loved Evie, hasn't he? And *will* always love her, yes? Great strong hand!"

And as she murmured thus, again I thought of Louie. It was with something like awe that I did so. "I think you'll find that sooner or later you've got to tell her." How did she know that? Did she know it? Had she foreseen how half-attempts would end, and known them beforehand to be wasted breath?

Then there came upon me the great need to see Louie again. I must see her, and quickly. With Evie still unenlightened, the actual perils of a meeting between herself and Kitty stood forward again, exactly as before. Evie herself might not now wish for such a meeting, but that would be on my account, and not that, if Kitty didn't mind, or positively wished it, she saw any reason against it. Why should she, if Kitty didn't?... Yes, I must see Louie again, at once. To-morrow was Sunday. I must see her on the Monday. I must write—telephone—do something——

"And to-morrow, Jeff," Evie was saying, with decision, "you really must have a walk. You're working yourself ill—you look worried to death. I can't come, of course, but I wish you'd go to Amersham or Chalfont or somewhere, just for a blow. Leave horrid business just for one day, and I'll have a nice supper ready for you when you come back. I shall be all right.... Hush! Listen!"

From upstairs had come a low, reedy cry.

"That's Jackie—I must fly! Don't sit down here, dear—come now——"

And she was off.

I followed her; and as I stood looking down on the boy, who had gone to sleep again of himself, I remembered my former dream, that by the wonder of an innocent birth atonement was to have come. I sighed. Apparently it hadn't.

Well, I must see Louie on the Monday, that was all.

III

I did see her on the Monday. I saw her at the models' Club, to which place I telephoned early on the Monday morning. I had the luck to get on to her immediately. "Yes?... This is Miss Causton," came the diminished voice over the wire; and she said she would see me that evening at seven. I sent Evie a message that I should be late.

Perhaps you know those premises in the Chelsea Square. Two houses have been thrown into one, but all I know of the establishment is the two rooms of the ground floor, which, barring a narrow passage with a rustling bead curtain across it, communicate. The room on the left of the curtain is a large bare apartment that is used for parties, tableaux, dancing and such like entertainments; that on the right is the tea-room, sewing and

The Debit Account

wardrobe room, and room for general purposes. At one end of it is a kitchener; placed near the kitchener is a small service counter, brass foot-rail and all, that has done duty in some saloon bar or other—it was probably picked up in the York Road, N.; and the furniture has been given piecemeal by artists and is characterised by great variety. The members can get tea for threepence halfpenny and dinner for eightpence; and of course I was Louie Causton's guest. She was looking out of the window as I approached the house; she herself opened the door to me; and we walked through the bead portière and entered the party-room on the left. We sat down by a yellow upright piano at the farther end of this room. I heard the frying of chops across the passage. They wouldn't be long, Louie said, and then added that I was looking pretty well.

A long walk round Chalfont Woods the previous day had, in fact, done me good. She herself appeared to be in excellent health and spirits. She asked me whether I had seen Billy Izzard lately, and then, without waiting for an answer, laughed as two girls, in waltzing attitude, balanced in the doorway for a moment, and then, seeing us, went out again. "The girls dance in here," Louie explained. "Oh, do you?" I remarked. "Oh, *I* don't," was her reply; and she went on to ask what was new with me. It was all refreshingly ordinary and matter-of-fact, and there was no indication that she had any serious care on her mind.

A stout woman in an apron appeared in the doorway and announced that our chops were ready. We passed into the other room. I said that the furniture of the Club had been given by artists; the table at which we sat down had been a card-table. As I could not get my legs under it I had to sit sideways at it, and our plates, cups and saucers were edge to edge, with the salt and pepper in the interstices. Louie smiled and said something about our interview being literally a tête-à-tête, and we attacked our chops.

From where I sat I could see the vista of the party-room across the passage, and Louie's eyes, as they met mine from time to time, had something of the same soft sheen of the polished floor of that apartment. She wore a navy blue skirt and plain white mercerised blouse without collar or any other finish at the neck; and as we ate and talked of this and that there rose in my mind again that surmise I had had when Billy had told me, by the Whitestone Pond, that she had stopped sitting. Nothing that I can describe happened to confirm that surmise, and yet somehow I was conscious of the growing confirmation. It had begun when she had twinkled and said, "How's Billy?" and a moment or two later, when the two girls had stood poised in the doorway for dancing, she had smiled and said, "Oh, *I* don't dance." The twinkle about Billy had not been lost on me; and when I tell you that the single dance of my own life had been with her, years before, at a breaking-up party at the old Business College, perhaps you can make a guess at the nature of my surmise.

For I had read in those eyes of hers, on that night of the Berkeley dinner, that she loved me and must go on loving me; and she herself had said, in so many words, "It's nothing to do with you—you can't help that." And now she had taken this fantastic resolution not to sit any more. Whether I would have it so or not, she had a right in me, in which, quite calmly and ordinarily, she now exulted. Yet had ever before mortal woman exulted over anything less substantial? The whole thing seemed to me both preposterously lovely and quite movingly absurd. She had wheedled out of Billy that perfect sketch that had stood on his easel that evening I had walked, unannounced, into his room opposite the Cobden Statue. Why? What ridiculous and sacred tapers did she burn about it? Billy must now paint her in costume or not at all. Why? Of what beautiful and empty union was this a consummation? Did she seriously intend that thenceforward no eye but mine—— But I waste words. You see it or you don't see it. That, as near as makes no matter, appeared to be how things stood between us, and there was nothing to tell me that she was not happy

The Debit Account

in this beautiful lunacy. As for myself, I supposed I must be content to be owned almost to the point of insult in possession.

"I'm just beginning to get used to it," I remember she said to me at one stage of that evening—the thing she was just beginning to get used to being sitting under the new conditions. "Did you know it was really harder? Your clothes tingle on you, you know."

I mention this only to show that, since she might speak at her pleasure of a thing of which I might not even recognise the existence, her tyranny over me was pretty complete.

We had finished our chops, and I was wondering what she supposed my reason for having sought her to be, when she herself put the direct question. She put her plate on the floor so as to make room for her elbows on the table.

"Give me a cigarette if you have one," she said. "I'm afraid I've picked up that habit here. All the girls do it: there's a cigarette-case in their bags if there's nothing else."

And when I had given her a light, she put her elbows on the table again, her wrists and forearms fell into an attitude that really made me sorrow for Billy, and she said: "Well, what is it?"

With no more waste of words than she herself had used, I told her of Miss Levey's voracious curiosity, of Evie's perplexed sense of something unexplained, and of my own unsuccessful attempt to have my eggs and my omelette too.

She listened attentively: the change of which I shall speak in a moment did not come all at once. Other girls had now come into the Club, and two or three of them were gathered about a brown-paper parcel, some purchase of dress material or other which they were discussing with animation. Others fetched cups of tea from the saloon bar counter, eating and drinking, perched carelessly on the ends of tables, the spiral twist of the work of their stockings telling how readily they got into and out of their clothes.

Before I had finished my story Louie interrupted me with the first of a little series of detached remarks.

"One moment," she said. "When do you start—this Consolidation, I mean?"

"In a few weeks. We shall send some of the men on in advance in about a fortnight. Why?"

"You don't intend to take Miriam Levey over with you?"

"I do not."

"You don't suppose she doesn't know that?"

"Well?"

"Well—but go on." She made a little gesture. "I interrupted you."

I went on.

"Half-a-minute," she came in again presently. "All this was quite—— I mean, there was no quarrel?"

"With Evie? No—oh, no, no."

"Well——"

And the next time she interrupted me was merely to ask me whether I had another cigarette.

I admit that there had come over me as I had talked an increasing sense of the burden I had placed upon her. Nor do I mean that I had not had this sense before. I had, indeed, thought of little else during my walk to Chalfont the previous day. But it is yet another coin added to the price of a righteous but unlicenced slaying that a man's selfishness becomes merely inordinate. I had known more or less what she must bear; exactly what she had to bear it with I had taken for granted. She had perhaps herself to thank for that, and that tense and incredible calm she had shown on the night I had dined at the Berkeley. I had known the depths of her womanliness that other night; soon I was to learn the shallows of her femininity.

"Well," she said, when at last I had finished, "I really don't see what else you expected. And," she went on, but more slowly, and somehow as if she didn't quite trust herself, "I don't see either what you expect of me. I told you what I thought before."

"You mean that I should have to tell her?"

"Yes."

"Well, tell me why."

"You've just told me why."

"Well, put it another way. You see the frightful risk—to her. The question is, ought it to be taken?"

For a moment those tourmalines of her eyes seemed to flicker, as if she would have shown me again the abysses beyond them; but they remained shut as she spoke more slowly still.

"That's not quite the question. Can you—go on—as you are doing? And if you can't, what's the alternative?"

To that I had no answer to make.

Her cigarette had gone out, and her beautiful fingers were holding it listlessly. All at once I found myself noticing the contrast between her and the chattering group of models down the room. The girl with the brown-paper parcel had approached a cupboard and taken out some second-hand property or other of frayed velvet and torn gold: "It's hardly worth re-making: I vote we cut it up," I heard her say. And I wondered whether Louie had sat in the torn and tawdry thing—now that she had been warned against chills. The giggling and the skiddle of teacups went on, but Louie pressed her fingers on her eyeballs for a moment. Perhaps it was this pressure that made them, when she looked up again, seem dull and tired.

"At any rate, that's how it strikes me," she said.

She looked suddenly older—much older—so much older that it gave me a pang. During my walk on the previous day I had told myself over and over again that I must have made of her life also exactly what I had made of my own—a fearful thing without trifles; but I had *had* to tell myself, if you appreciate what I mean. Now, to see it with my own eyes was another matter. There was that other quantity, the quantity unknown to me but drearily familiar enough to her, I didn't doubt—Kitty.... A word of advice to those who contemplate the putting out of a life on their own responsibility: When a woman, on a rainy night in St. James's Park, or wherever and whenever, lets you look down into her soul, and drops a plummet into your own, and asks you whether you are not a murderer, and you no more dare to lie than you would dare a foulness in the face of majesty, then do anything you like—fly from her, bite out your tongue, kill her also—but for mere pity of her don't answer "Yes." Don't, that is, unless you are sure that she will betray you. If you do, depend on it she'll ask you to a Models' Club or somewhere, and the horror of a life without trifles will come over you, and you'll see her press her fingers on her eyeballs and then look up again, five years older in as many minutes.

"What about Kitty?" I asked abruptly.

She answered quickly—too quickly: "Oh, Kitty's all right; you needn't bother about Kitty; leave her to me. As a matter of fact she's been awfully useful to me."

"How useful?"

The Debit Account

"Oh, in quite the most material way," she said, with a short and mirthless laugh. "That's not been pure philanthropy, I assure you. I dare say you know——"

I did know that Kitty had perhaps a pound a week of her own money, from some tramways out Edgbaston way.

"And she types at home, too—authors' manuscript—when she can get it—and I save the ten shillings I had to pay somebody to look after the boy."

"And you yourself?" I ventured meaningly.

"Oh," she answered evasively, "we've not stuck fast yet."

"In spite of your chills," thought I; and then, as another burst of laughter broke from the girls down the room, I said aloud: "Tell me—I've never asked you—how did you drop into this kind of thing? You used to be at a business college."

Again she smiled. "Did I? Sometimes I can hardly believe that was I. It's precious little I learned there, anyway. And this other—I could explain to Billy—I'm not pretty, I know, not my face, but—well, it seemed a fairly obvious thing to do. There wasn't much else, anyhow, and remember I did fairly well out of it—better than most girls in offices."

She had grown faintly pink, and again the tourmalines had given, as it were, a half turn. I dropped my voice and looked earnestly at her.

"And these—chills—aren't they anything you could ever grow out of?"

The soft irradiation deepened as she looked as earnestly back at me.

"No," she said.

"I see. And what you learned at the College—have you forgotten all that?"

Then, looking almost challengingly at one another, we began to speak rather quickly, and a little elliptically.

"I think I can guess what you mean," she said, dropping her gaze again.

"I think you do."

"That's why I asked you just now when the Consolidation was starting.... You don't suppose she'll love you any more for throwing her out of a job, do you?"

"She can't hate me much more than she does."

"Well, you may depend upon it, she knows she's going."

"Well, that saves trouble."

"Oh, no, it doesn't."

"Ah!—You think not?"

"I'm sure not."

A pause.

"I gather you've seen her?"

"Oh, often."

"At your place?"

"Yes."

"I don't suppose you love her much. Why do you have her there?"

"You don't love her either. Why do you?"

"Well, there's Evie."

"And there's Kitty."

Another pause, and then: "I see."

The Debit Account

Then suddenly I spoke a little more to the point.

"Well, would you accept the job if I could arrange it?"

She hesitated. "It's very necessary, of course, that I should do something."

"You'd take it?"

"I almost think—there's my boy, you see—but we'll talk about that in a minute. You were asking me about Kitty. I don't think you need worry about her. I keep her in hand. I don't think it would matter very much if she and your wife did meet, and, on the whole, you'd be doing more harm by objecting beyond a certain point than you would by allowing it. So, as far as she's concerned, things had better drift. The worst of it is"—again the fingers on the eyeballs—"they don't drift."

"Don't drift?"

"You know what Miriam Levey is."

I caught my breath. "You don't mean *she's* any idea——" I said quickly.

"Oh, none whatever," Louie said hurriedly. "I don't mean that at all. But I *do* mean she'd thoroughly enjoy seeing you made uncomfortable—got at—scored off—get her own back—you know what I mean."

"That's noth——" I began absently, but checked myself. "That's nothing," I had been on the point of saying, but there were no nothings for us. Louie's vigils must be as unremitting as my own.

Suddenly I found myself without the heart to ask her in detail what these were. We now had the tea-room to ourselves; the bevy of models had scurried off to the party-room, and two of them appeared to be playing an elementary duet on the piano, with wrong notes loudly and laboriously corrected, amid laughter and general high spirits. Again the contrast was cruel. *They* hadn't to look before, behind and about them for the dread of a ruinous inadvertence.... You will find it difficult to reconcile with remorse, by the way, that, stealing another glance at Louie's drawn and anxious face, I cursed a heedless young cub who had gone to his account nearly six years before.

"Anyway," she said, after a long silence, "I'll see to that as far as I can. Plan as we like, we've got to take some risks. Don't look at me like that. It isn't more than I can bear. There's joy in it too. The only thing I don't quite understand is why *I* should want to throw that joy away by—by giving you the advice I did."

"The advice you did?"

"To tell your wife."

"But——" It broke agitatedly from me. Again the tourmalines seemed to move.

"The risk; just so; don't think I don't see it. Oh, I see it—far more plainly than you do! Haven't you thought that perhaps it's that that——" She stopped abruptly, ending in a little twanging murmur.

And I had at last become conscious of something that hitherto I had only half consciously noticed—namely, that she spoke of Evie repeatedly as "your wife." Obstinately she refused to use her name. I think that I felt even then our approach to what I have called the shallows of her femininity. Can you wonder at it? Is it so very surprising that, with the tremors of those shut transmitters of her eyes, the whole fantastic and exhausting fabric of my interpretation of her feeling for myself tottered? He has to be a greater painter than Billy Izzard whose fiction can fill the life of a woman already past thirty, whom you have so heaped with cares that her face takes on age as you look at it! Her voice shook as she strove to hide all this from me.

The Debit Account

"But you see the disadvantage you have me at," she said. "*You* know what you really want, though you haven't put it quite plainly yet; but even if I were to try it you wouldn't let me say what *I* mean."

"Oh, say it, say it: we're in the mess, and it's no good keeping things back."

"No, no—you've no right to expect that of me. I'll do everything else, but I'm only a mortal woman, with limbs and hungers, after all."

"You're a very wondrous one."

"Tch!" The exclamation broke from her as if I had blundered on a nerve with an instrument. "You're making big demands of my wondrousness, Jim!"

I gave a low groan. "Poor woman! Is it more than——"

But she broke out into quite a loud cry.

"Not that, Jim," she commanded, "not—that! That's the only thing I will *not* bear! If you're going to make me out noble, or disinterested, or self-sacrificing, or anything of that sort I—I can't bear it. I'm not. I hate Evie. I hate myself. I almost hate you when I see how stupid and clumsy you can be. Oh, *you* know what *you* want! You want just one thing—to be happy with her; but do you think I scheme and contrive for you because *I* want you to be happy with her? Oh no! I do it because I can't help myself, and because it's that or nothing between you and me, and that's all there is splendid about it! I won't be called 'Poor woman.' And you needn't shake your head either. If I could get you, I would; but there it is, I can't, and that's all the loyalty I have for *her*! And you ask me," she broke out anew, almost furiously, "you ask me whether I 'don't see' things! It's you who don't see, and never will! You get a fixed idea into your head, and everything else——" She snapped her fingers. "What do you suppose your wife would say if she knew you were here with me now? *I* shouldn't care a straw about her knowing, but have you told *her*? *Will* you tell her? You know you won't! You daren't—you daren't trust her! Oh, I know what you're going to say—that you can't discuss her with me—but in that case you shouldn't take my position quite so much for granted. I'm the last person to put on a pedestal. You ask me whether I see things: don't I! Don't I see what they might have been—yes, even in spite of the mess I made of them! With half a chance I could have——"

"Louie!"

"Sssh—it's got to come out now! I was happy till that night—you know the night I mean—and that night I was fool enough to think it was possible to stop up there—away up in the air. I gave you and got from you that night what no other woman on earth could have done, and I thought we could stop at that. I thought I could go on living at that. I thought that would be enough for me; and when I found it wasn't, I began to—bolster it up. You've seen Billy—you know what I mean. And I still have something of you that nobody else has, and—I want to give it away! I want you to give her that too! I advise you to tell her and leave me with nothing! I must be mad! Jim"—her voice dropped with startling effect—"you once said that to tell her would be to kill her: *if I could only think that*!... But there, you'll tell her, and take away the last thing I have of you.... But she won't get that thing. It's beyond her. That's yours and mine whether you wish it or not. If you don't believe me, try it. Tell her. Tell her her husband made away with her sweetheart; tell her why; tell her what you've told me, and if she takes it as I did, I haven't another word to say. I hate her; I'm not running away from that; so perhaps I'm not just. Perhaps there is a chance: if so, it's your only one. I've had no luck. I'm out of it, and there's no more to say. Give me a match."

She took up and relighted her half-smoked cigarette.

I have merely set down what she said, and the way she said it; for the rest, I leave you to draw your own conclusions. Perhaps it is unusual to allow these freedoms to be taken with your wife, but I think you will admit that the occasion was unusual. She had told me, in effect, that murderers ought to be careful whom they marry, and that I had married the wrong woman: but she had left out of the account one thing that made all the difference. You know as well as I what she had left out—the supreme sanctification of the flesh: "With my body I thee worship."... It was Evie, not Louie Causton, with whom I had heard that nightingale sing on Wimbledon Common. They had been Evie's lips, not Louie's, that had not sought to escape my own on that September evening in Kensington Gardens. It was Evie whom I had married.... It was natural that Louie should see how things might conceivably have been different; you can say that however they turn out; and perhaps that was where the fatality came in. Circumstance, propinquity, accident, a step rightly or wrongly taken, and the rest is predicated with a terrible inevitability. Louie had had no luck; and now, not because I had placed a crushing weight upon her, but because I had given her the pity while another got the love, she had broken out upon me.

At any rate, I saw her own position sadly clearly now.

And, there being no more to say, she rose.

In the hall, however, she did find one more word to say. They were playing Sir Roger in the party-room as I held aside the bead *portière* for Louie to pass, and the couples, seen through the gauzy hanging, seemed spectrally charming. Louie stood on the other side of the curtain, mortal, unspectral enough under a cheap square hall lamp with tesseræ of coloured glass. With head downhung, she moved spiritlessly towards the outer door, where she stood meditatively with her hand on the letter-box. At last she looked up.

"About what you were saying about Miriam Levey," she said, without preface. "I don't think it would do—not now."

I knew she meant her own acceptance of Miriam's place. I asked her why not.

"Oh, I've said too much for that to be possible now. We've been too near. We mustn't come so near again."

"But surely," I said dispiritedly, "a job——"

She shook her head. "I should be seeing you," she said. "It wouldn't do. Good-night."

And I lost the strains of Sir Roger as the door closed between us.

IV

Looking back over what I have written, I find it will hasten my tale if I take events with rather a free hand in point of time, sequence and so forth; and I shall do so. For example, the setting up of the Consolidation in Pall Mall did not actually take place until the following spring, but our arrangements were complete long before that time, and, as my tale is about myself rather than about the Consolidation, I will say as much as is necessary about that enterprise now, and have done with it.

We have to all intents and purposes absorbed the old F.B.C., and this has been greatly to the advantage of both concerns. The Company's mercantile position is the firmer, and we are left the freer for things both larger and more special. In the handling of these Pepper has been brilliant. True, he has taken chances, sometimes more than I have liked;

but he is a born taker of chances, and it is astonishing, on the whole, how seldom things have failed to come off. In his own line I have never met his equal. I think I mentioned that he had been in Russia: I never knew exactly what his errand was there; but I can make a guess at the kind of thing. Last summer, for instance, he was out in the West Indies—with a few tin specimen-boxes and a butterfly net (this is the man who doesn't know a butterfly from a bumble-bee, and once asked me what a birch was). Out in the West Indies he met Magnay, of Astbury, Phillips—a valetudinarian after tarpon. Sichel was there too; I forget whether he was playing golf, or healing a lung, or merely yawning his head off in deck-chairs. And of course (a nod being as good as a wink to a blind horse) there could be no possible connection between these innocent pursuits and the Panama Canal, trans-shipment stations and the South American coasting trade.... So maybe Pepper had had no thought of hides or timber or tallow when he had learned the Siberian method of hunting bear.... Anyway, all I want you to understand, without making it too plain, is that we leave these things to Pepper. He dines geologists and botanists and explorers and concessionaires: he does them well, and is perfectly charming; and it may quite well be that, before he has finished with them, a little inconspicuous piece of paper that not one in a thousand as much as glances at is posted up in Whitehall one day, Britain has proclaimed a new Protectorate somewhere or other, and the Consolidation is at the bottom of it. It pays us that Pepper keeps his nails manicured and knows his way about a wine-list. It may not be noble or altruistic or anything of that kind, but it's the way things get done in this world, and be hanged to Schmerveloff and the humanitarians.

So, while we were still with the F.B.C., Pepper was playing every ball straight back to the inquisitive folk who wanted to know what was in the wind, we were ready to go over at a month's notice to that great new cathedral of a place with the mosaic floors and the bronze statues in the niches, and I was free to rub my rosy prospects into Aunt Angela to my heart's content. It had come off, or, thanks to Pepper and Robson and the rest of them, could hardly now fail to do so. But Aunt Angela, when I twinkled at her, and mentioned this, only gave me back my smiles thrice spiritualised. She never failed to rejoice, for our sakes, whenever a new piece of furniture came into the house in Well Walk, but for herself, her attitude was piously and amusingly penitential. I never knew austerity so resemble luxuriousness—or the other way about, whichever it was. And of this new furniture we presently began to have quite a lot. Collecting, as I have since come to understand the word, was as yet, of course, far beyond my means; but I used a bronze copy of a lioness by Barye on my desk as a paper-weight, I had good autotypes of Méryon on my study walls, I had bought Evie a dinner service, quite good enough for most occasions even to-day, and I had sales' catalogues and auctioneers' circulars, a dozen a week. Oh, yes, we were getting on, and Pepper winked, remembering his candlesticks, but said nothing.

But let me return to Aunt Angela for a moment. The effect on her of these evidences of our increasing prosperity was curious. Without the loss of a jot of her amiability, but rather to the increase of it, she set herself apart from our modest splendours. If I use the word "religiosity" I mean it only in its most innocent sense: but something of the sort had been incipient in her for a long time, and now merely became declared. Perhaps I cannot do better than tell here of the evening in which I first discovered how far this had gone. If at this point my narrative seems a little diffuse, it is merely because the longest way round is often the shortest way home, and also because Aunt Angela's attitude was not the only thing I learned that night.

I think it would be a little before Christmas, on a Tuesday or Wednesday; I know the day, if not the week, because it was what Evie, who corrected some of my own recklessnesses by still clinging to small economies, called an "eating-up night." On those

The Debit Account

nights I was expressly forbidden to bring anybody home to dinner—I except Aunt Angela and Billy Izzard, who came when they pleased. As it happened, they had both turned up on that very evening, and had partaken of a rather scratch supper; and I, who had had an exceptionally heavy day, hoped that nobody would come in afterwards—not that anybody was very likely to. As Jackie had gone to bed, Billy had been allowed to play Evie's new piano only with the soft pedal down (Evie herself, I may say, did not play, but was resolved to learn); and Aunt Angela had several skeins of wool to wind into balls. From the arm-chair in which I half dozed I could see Evie, still in the waterproof apron in which she had given Jackie his bath, setting the child's basket to rights. Our only maid was taking her "evening out" and was probably up on the Spaniards Road.

I was not too sleepy to see that Aunt Angela needed somebody to hold her wool, and I volunteered drowsily for the service. But, "No, thanks, Jeff," she replied; "you have a nap; besides, I must be getting used to doing things for myself." I did not insist, and the last thing I remember before I dropped off for forty winks was seeing her reach for Pepper's candlesticks, place them on the hearthrug, and, passing a hank of wool about them, begin to wind.

It seemed to me that several sounds awoke me simultaneously—the stopping of a hansom at the front door, the ringing of a bell downstairs, and a quick exclamation from Evie. It was not impossible, of course, that any one of a number of visitors might have called in a hansom at half-past nine at night, but Evie had concluded, and rightly as it happened, that this was the one with whom she was least of all at home—Pepper. I heard her suppressed exclamation of "Bother!" The next moment she had whisked off the waterproof apron, thrust it under the piano lid, then, seeing Aunt Angela still placidly winding, had said, "Quick—in case—hide them, Auntie," and had flown to answer the bell.

But Aunt Angela, in her flurry, had only succeeded in making the candlesticks a hopeless cat's-cradle of wool before Evie's voice of vivacious welcome was heard, and Pepper himself entered.

He had Whitlock and a stranger with him, the latter a bearded and taciturn provincial who was introduced as Mr Toothill. Mr Toothill, indeed, I gathered to be the reason of the visit. Pepper has to be charming to a great variety of men, and is not often beaten, but occasionally there does fall to him ("for his virtues," he says) a man he can neither dine, wine nor take to a show, and I know the signs in him when he is at his most affable and most intensely bored. I may say at once that Mr Toothill has no connection with my tale other than as having been the cause of this visit.

Now Pepper has the gift of being able to make all manner of things (especially men) invisible when he chooses; and although Aunt Angela, in making out of sight with the wool and the candlesticks of Pepper's own giving, had only succeeded in putting them on the table and making them the most conspicuous objects in the room, for Pepper they did not exist. That bright photographic eye of his took in every other object in the room, but no candlesticks.

But not so Mr Toothill. He came, Whitlock told me afterwards, from the West Riding of Yorkshire, where he was a power; but so little of a power was he in London that, had Pepper not rashly burdened himself with him, he would probably have waited in King's Cross Station for the next train back to his own parts. Anyway, here he was in my house, and as his eyes fell on the wool-winding, they lighted up (so Whitlock said) with the first spark of interest they had shown that evening.

"This is like ho-o-ome, at all events," he said, giving the word I don't know how many "o's." "But you've got it felted, haven't you? If the ladies will excuse me———"

The Debit Account

And without more ceremony, and in spite of Aunt Angela's protestations, he drew the candlesticks towards himself, began to unravel the ridiculous tangle, and became for purposes of conversation a piece of furniture with a beard.

Of course Mr Toothill had been foisted on us merely because Pepper had not known what else in the world to do with him; but Pepper's beautiful candour rarely confessed much of what was really passing in his mind, and I awaited with relish the reason he would give for his call. By this time I was quite wide awake again; and Mr Toothill had refused the whisky I had got out.

Well, Judy had several reasons, all sufficient, all perfect; but alas! he and Evie ever hit it off with deplorable lucklessness. He and Whitlock were Jackie's godfathers; but, as against the rather loud way in which he had rung the bell, his urbanities about the spiritual relationship availed him little with Evie. Her looks said plainly, to me at all events, that if Pepper intended her to believe that he had called on an eating-up night merely to ask how Jackie was getting on, he mistook her. Driven from this outpost, Pepper proudly refused to urge the commonplace excuse of private business with myself. Instead, he delicately adjusted his trousers, produced his cigar-case, besought Evie's permission with a glance, and then, lighting up with deliberation, astonished myself hardly less than Evie by saying: "Well—unless Whitlock's already told you—I've come for your congratulations, Mrs Jeffries."

"Oh? What on, Mr Pepper?" said Evie. She had summoned up a ready, glad look.

"Ah, I see he hasn't told you. Stupid of me—of course he couldn't have, as I only heard myself about four hours ago. Dear Mrs Jeffries, you may congratulate me on my impending knighthood."

Evie jumped up. "*Really?*" I myself was not so much surprised at the fact as at the moment of its coming, though my surprise at that also passed instantly. Of course it would be so much prestige for the Consolidation.

Yes, Judy was down among the approaching New Year's Honours. And so he ought to have been. If there is official recognition for a man who can merely advise in a party's interest which provincial mayors can be given the accolade without being made the laughing-stock of their neighbours, Judy's services to the Administration had been far greater. To the man on 'change this would doubtless seem a feather in the cap of the F.B.C.; only a few knew that before long it would prove a thorn in their sides. Yes, it was distinctly good preparation for the coming Consolidation, and, in the meantime, there was the knight-elect's health to drink, and I had only got the whisky out. I myself fetched up the claret for Aunt Angela and Evie. Both the announcement and the manner of it had been a huge success, and Billy Izzard, remarking "I won't say 'may I,'—" reached for Pepper's cigar-case.

"Well, I *am* glad!" said Evie, maybe, wife-like, casting ahead in a wonder as to what my own chances might be. "And are we really the first to know?"

"Except Whitlock and Mr Toothill, yes. But of course I needn't say——"

"Oh, of course we wouldn't breathe a word! Isn't it splendid, auntie?"

Indeed, Evie seemed quite won over. I think she came nearer that evening to liking Pepper than she has done either before or since.

As I said, I have an object in relating all this—several objects. The next thing happened perhaps half-an-hour later, when Mr Toothill had almost freed one candlestick of wool, but otherwise had not greatly added to our sociability. For that half hour Pepper had reigned among us, but then, bit by bit, he had begun slowly to slip back again. We had guardedly discussed the prospects of the Consolidation; and then, as a preliminary to his coming down presently with a run, Pepper made a perfectly innocent but altogether luckless remark. It was about Miss Levey.

The Debit Account

"It was understood she wasn't to come over," he grumbled; "I agreed to that; but I don't see why she should be taken away from me just now." (I had got rid of Miss Levey that very week.) "Hang her private convictions! What do I care about her private convictions as long as she does her work?"

I laughed, though a little lamely. "My dear Judy, we don't want a woman whose job interferes with her propaganda, and she's been incubating 'rights' of one sort and another for a long time. Send her to Schmerveloff: he receives that sort with open arms. Let him make a case of persecution out of it. We want efficiency."

"But, dash it all, she *was* efficient."

"She wasn't. You had to pull her up last week, and I had twice the week before. She'd been warned."

Judy, who really didn't care a button about the loss of Miss Levey, laughed. "The red rag again, Jeffries! You have here, Mr Toothill, quite the most insular man in this realm, *and* the most obstinate. I can make him do anything he's a mind to—and not much else. Well, well, if you won't have a suffragette, perhaps you'll find me a member of the Women's Primrose League?"

But here Whitlock struck in. "By the way, I'd an applicant this morning."

"From the Women's Primrose League?" Pepper tossed over his shoulder.

"I don't mean for the private work, but as general amanuensis," Whitlock went on. "I asked her how she heard we wanted anybody, and she said she hadn't—had just looked in on the chance."

"Go to Jeffries, since he's made it his affair," Pepper grumbled.

"Well, Miss Day *is* getting married," Whitlock went on, "so that we shall want somebody in the outer office. Then promote Miss Lingard——"

"What was she like?"

Billy Izzard's eyes were dreamily on the smoke of Pepper's expensive cigar, but I saw a change come into them. Whitlock has a passable gift of description. He began to describe the woman who had looked in on the chance of a job: before he had finished I had no doubt, and Billy (I gathered) not much, of who the female out-o'-work had been. "Hallo, my model!" I guessed to be in his mind; but it was no business of his, and he appeared to be relishing his cigar as before.

"I've forgotten her name, but I have it in the book," Whitlock concluded. "Clouston or Christian or something like that."

"Well, see she isn't anti-suffrage either," quoth Pepper; "as far as I can see, that would be just as bad."

And he selected a fresh cigar.

My first thought had shaped itself in the very words for which Louie herself had pulled me up so sharply: "Poor woman!" For it was pathetically clear what had happened—what must have happened. Once more she had taken a resolution too heroic to be held to, and whether she had caved in because of myself or because of the necessity for feeding and clothing her boy made no practical difference. I could only hope it was the last. Poverty leaves little room for heroics. Later, as I think I told you, Louie got Miss Day's post, and after that Miss Lingard's, which she has still.

And my second thought was that, as she had applied of herself for Miss Levey's place, there would now be no more love lost between her and Miss Levey than there was between Miss Levey and myself. I began to muse on this....

But let me go on with that curiously broken evening.

75

Ever since Pepper had told us about his knighthood Aunt Angela had sat, her slender fingers folded in her lap, smiling from time to time into the fire. Now knighthood is a temporal distinction, and, as such (I am putting this bluntly), another nut for that new and dainty humility of hers to crack. For worldliness, it was my own promised wealth in another form; and against such things she seemed to have taken up some sort of a position. I think the less practicable human charities had given her a tenderness even for Miss Levey, for I had not escaped a soft look of reproach when I had made my observations on that lady; and altogether she appeared to be wrapped in a little private veil of dissociation from the rest of us and our doings.

So—again to anticipate what became plain a little later—she also was nursing her little surprise for us. Several times during the last month or two she had spoken vaguely of leaving her rooms in Woburn Place, the rooms she had shared with Evie before our marriage; but I had not taken her very seriously; she was welcome to come to us (as she afterwards did) whenever she chose, and she knew it. But she had got it into her head that she would like to take a single room—oh, quite a large, airy, cheerful one—and, as it turned out presently, she had actually done so that very day.

Some chance remark of Pepper's—I think it was something about how pleasant it was to see us thus in our little family circle—gave her the opportunity for her announcement. There had been a little byplay between Pepper and Evie, who had wanted to know why in that case he didn't get married himself; and to that Pepper, abolishing (as it were) the candlesticks under his nose by an act equal in potency to that of creation itself, had answered gallantly (and, in the presence of those candlesticks, rather naughtily) that our own ménage set him a standard which he would rather cherish in thought than fall from in miserable actuality. It was then that his look embraced Aunt Angela, and my maiden aunt by marriage smiled.

"I suppose Mr Pepper thinks I live here because he always finds me here," she said. "But that's only because I've no conscience about inflicting myself on other people. *My* dwelling's a much more modest one than this, Mr Pepper."

I think Pepper was insincere enough to reply that that it might quite well be and yet almost everything that could be desired.

"I forgot to tell you that, Jeff," Aunt Angela continued, turning to me. "As a matter of fact I only settled the matter to-day—so you're not the only one for whom to-day's been *quite* important, Mr Pepper." She preened herself.

"Oh!" I said shortly. I thought the whole idea rather stupid. But she continued:

"I go in in exactly ten days, as soon as the paint's dry. And as I don't begin to pay till Christmas, I actually get a week for nothing. That might not be much to some people," she purred, dropping her eyes, "but it's quite a lot to me. So, Jeff, I shall want you to bring a hammer and a foot-rule—or whatever it is. He's *so* clever at putting up things, Mr Pepper."

She ran amiably on, describing her proposed arrangements.

I could hardly blame Pepper that, to save himself from talking, he drew her out. He was bored to death with the drowsy banality of the evening. So Aunt Angela told us how cosy she was going to be in her new quarters. With her bed screened off in one corner, and the day's fire still burning, she would be able (she said) to lie happily awake and watch the firelight on the ceiling and indulge "an old woman's fancies"; there would be no stairs except when she came out of doors; and she wouldn't have to cook in the same room, for there was a little landing with a stove left by the last tenant—and so on. Pepper was the picture of polite interest.

"And I shall give a little housewarming, I think," she said, as one who knew that hospitality consisted in the hostship and not in the entertainment provided. "Really I should like to ask you all, Mr Toothill too."

Toothill, who had now finished the "unfelting," had struck a match and was experimenting to find out how much of the worsted was cotton and how much wool. He looked up for a moment, but resumed his occupation. Pepper hoped that *he* would not be left out of Aunt Angela's housewarming.

Aunt Angela murmured that that was very sweet of him.

And the smallest of small talk went on.

I don't know that I need give any more of it. Indeed, I don't remember any more of it. Toothill found the wool to be "sixty Botany" or something of the kind, and we sat on, everybody wanting to break the party up, but nobody (not even Pepper) knowing quite how to do so without an open reference to a watch. I omit the details of Pepper's complete downfall in Evie's eyes. I know that by some accident or other the piano lid was opened, displaying the waterproof apron, and that poor Evie, flurried until she hardly knew what she was saying, committed the solecism of calling Pepper "Sir Julius," grew pink (poor dear), and hated, not herself, but Pepper. Also her frugality received a shock when it was discovered that the hansom had been kept waiting all this time. Then the maid, returning from the Spaniards Road, filled my poor wife's cup by bringing in I know not what homely provision for Jackie's comfort during the night. Then they went.

Now, except when the flattery of personal attention is of the highest importance, Pepper turns all provincials over to Whitlock; and I myself, if ever Mr Toothill turns up at my house again, shall take the precaution of having a whole barrow-load of worsted for his entertainment, and if possible a kitten to "felt" it for him.

V

I have now to tell how Aunt Angela was as good as her word about the housewarming of her new abode. I hope that in these last pages I have not seemed harsh in thought to the kind and aimless soul. She did not meditate the mischief that came of that evening, and it was not for lack of anything she was able to do to remedy it afterwards that partial, if not total shipwreck came. But that helped little. Malevolence, in my experience, is not the worst of dangers a man as exposed as I has to fear. It is the mischief hat grows as it were of itself, inherent in persons and their diverse characters and manifold relations that is the deadly thing. That is not mere bad luck; it is fatality, and there is no defeating it. I myself was so specially open to it that to all intents and purposes I might as well have gone skinless through the world.... Well, I grinned and bore it. Only one other person knew that I was skinless, and she, alas, was skinless too. Oh, take it on my authority if you cannot take it otherwise, that you will do wisely to keep out of my predicament unless you are of a different temper from mine, have skins to spare, or are prepared to endure the shock I was presently to endure.

I made no attempt to see that other skinless person. If she had found herself driven, from need or any other consideration, to seek a job with the Consolidation, so much the worse; I did not see that that released me from anything she had laid upon me. In any case, as Miss Day's successor, I should rarely see her; even did she pass to the place

The Debit Account

lately held by Miss Lingard I should, no doubt, be able to avoid her; and for the rest, as she herself had said, things must drift. Sometimes, if I must confess the truth, I found myself getting quite childishly petulant about her. Why had she given me to suppose she was something she wasn't? Why had she let me see her all caught-up and wise and able to bear, as she had shown herself on that first memorable night, and then gone to pieces like this? *I* couldn't have known her private feelings, but *she* must have known them....

And what kind of impossible situation was going to be created if, even avoiding other intercourse, I had to encounter those tourmalines of her eyes every time I passed through the busy office to Pepper's room?

So sometimes I forgot what I had laid upon her, and was callous enough and harassed enough to entertain almost a weak resentment against her.

Aunt Angela's new dwelling was in one of those curiously secluded little squares or "circuses" that lie immediately east of King's Cross Road in the neighbourhood of Mount Pleasant. You turn up from the squalid shops and public-houses and trams, and the length of a short steep street brings you into a space with well-built houses about it, trees and birds in the middle, and long narrow gardens with apple and plum and pear at the back. Away to the north the heights of Hampstead seem positively precipitous, and, looking the other way, the multitude of turrets and towers and spires, with St Paul's reigning over them all, is singularly inspiring. Aunt Angela's rooms were very advantageously placed for both these prospects. The first time I went she took me up a breakneck ladder, through a square trapdoor in which I almost stuck fast, and out on to the leads. The sky, torn in primrose-coloured rents and all smoke-browned, was very stormy and fine; and Aunt Angela was looking forward to taking tea out on the roof when the summer came.

"And I shall be able to look away to where my dear ones are," she said, looking north again.

Her room was immediately under this flat roof. It had two windows which looked on the trees in front, and, at the half turn of the stairs, a third which gave on the grimy back garden. In this garden poultry scratched; but there really was a plum-tree, and also a fig that had been known to bear. Her bed, being convertible into a couch by day, did not require to be screened off after all, and the tiny fireplace had brown tiles and a blackleaded iron kerb. One peculiarity the apartment had which I ought to mention: this was a large enclosed cistern, which by rights ought to have been on the roof outside. It held the water supply for the whole house, and as the ball inside it rose and sank, its sounds varied from a gentle tinkling to a soft whispering; the sounds never quite ceased. A stout post some feet from the wall supported one corner of this cistern, and this Aunt Angela, or rather I for her, converted into a hatstand.

It was as she handed me the four black hooks and the paper of screws for this purpose one evening that the sound of the cistern sank to a hissing. "Oh, do give a look to it," she said; "perhaps it wants a washer or something: you can reach it from the window-ledge. And oh, dear, I've got the screws but no screwdriver! There have been hooks in before, haven't there? You'll have to put these higher up then. I'll see if I can borrow a screwdriver downstairs; but see to the cistern first."

But there was nothing to be done with the cistern; if she stayed there she would have to get used to it, that was all. I went up from Pall Mall several evenings to see to her installation, but I never imagined she would stay there very long. The place looked too suddenly cosy when the fire was lighted and the tea-table brightly set.

And so I put her the hooks and a shelf or two up, and made her as comfortable as I could.

Then one night, just as she was settling down, I went in about something or other and found Miss Levey and Aschael there. They seemed to have come for the evening, for

78

The Debit Account

their hats were on the hooks on the cistern post. Miss Levey appeared to have forgotten that I had virtually forbidden her my house and turned her out of her job as well; as we shook hands anybody might have supposed that we were the best of friends. She and Aunt Angela appeared to be on quite affectionate terms; and I gathered that Miss Levey was giving lessons by post in secretarial work and doing quite well out of it. Her passing over by the Consolidation she spoke of as a resignation. She was planning to link up her Commercial Correspondence Class with some Guild or other for the Economic Emancipation of Women, and wanted to tell me all about it. I did not stay long.

And of course I couldn't choose Aunt Angela's associates for her.

At first I had refused to go to that party of Aunt Angela's. I had grounds enough for my refusal, for we live half our lives two or three years ahead at the Consolidation, and there were clouds on the economic horizon. Men who live what I may call "short-date" lives can provide for contingencies as they arise, but the surveyor of the future, though he may know things to be inevitable, must be prepared, not for one way in which they may come about, nor even for the most probable way, but for all possible ways. Any one of a thousand symptomatic occurrences may make the Consolidation's most elaborate plans of yesterday of no avail, and work is ten times work when this happens. It had happened several times lately, and but for Pepper's marvellous resilience, my own capacity for long spells of forced labour, and the invaluable inertia of administrative departments, it would have proved too much for us.

I can honestly say that, full of these preoccupations, I had not been influenced by the fact that in all probability Aschael and Miss Levey would be there. I had forgotten all about them.

But Evie's look of resignation when I had told her that I was not going had touched me. We now knew quite a number of people, some of them quite charming people too; and while Evie made less use of this advantage than I could sometimes have wished, I couldn't reproach her for being faithful to her older friends. For a long time we had not been anywhere together. Therefore, seeing her patient yet fallen face, I had promised to make an effort at least to fetch her away, and to arrive earlier if possible. Her instant brightening had amply repaid me.

The party was given on a sharp night towards the end of January, and, try as I would, I had been unable to leave Pall Mall before half-past nine. I should have liked to walk, but that would have taken nearly three-quarters of an hour, and so, near the old F.B.C., I had hailed a hansom. "King's Cross, and then I'll tell you," I had said to the driver; and as I had sped along Holborn and up Judd Street I had relapsed into consideration of the affairs of the day again. The stopping of the hansom and the lifting of the trap aroused me. I gave the man the name of a chapel, and bade him then take a turning to the left; and we went forward again. We passed up a short, steep street at a walk, and stopped in the little "circus."

Aunt Angela's two front windows were lighted and open at the top, and as I paid off my cabman sounds of a nasal singing floated out. I ascended the steps and rang twice—Aunt Angela's signal; but I had to give the double ring again, so merry were they making upstairs. Then I heard steps descending. They were a man's steps, and I gave a sort of mental nod when Aschael opened the door. I had thought he would be there.

"Ve'd about given you up," he said familiarly. "Come in, von't you?"

I followed Aschael upstairs.

It would not greatly have surprised me had Miss Levey taken it upon herself to receive me, as her *fiancé* (if he was her *fiancé*; I never knew) had made me welcome downstairs;

but Aunt Angela, trying to appear calm, but really one flutter of pleasure at the success of her little party, met me at the door.

"How late you are," she said gaily. "Yes, yes—I know you'd have come sooner if you could. I'm not scolding you. Now I expect you're hungry; you must have some supper first, and then you shall be introduced to anybody you don't know. Mr Aschael, you'll get him all he wants, won't you?"

"Vith pleasure, Miss Angela," said Aschael, bustling about, all hands and smiles and ringlets.

Along the wall to my right, as I entered, ran a table, spread with the disarray of a quite elaborate supper. Plates were littered with banana skins, grape-twigs with the tiny morsels of pulp still on them, broken biscuits and remnants of jelly; and beyond this table, under the cistern in the corner, was a smaller one, with half a frilled ham, the wreckage of a tongue and a severely mutilated cold pie. Several flasks of colonial Burgundy had been opened; syphons stood among these; and from that secret and inexhaustible hoard of her belongings Aunt Angela had unearthed quite a large number of wineglasses, red ones, green ones, and some of clear glass. Nay, the entertainment had even run into a large box of Christmas crackers; the coloured paper and bright gelatine of these lay scattered among the plates; and my first impression of the number of people who made the room very warm was that half of them had flimsy tissue-paper caps and bonnets on their heads.

But, as I happened to be more than a little hungry, I merely sketched a sort of general and inclusive bow, sat down, and allowed Aschael to wait on me.

Then, my hunger appeased, I began to look about me.

That the gathering was too large for Aunt Angela's not very large room I instinctively set down to Miss Levey's account, for several of those present appeared to be her friends. There must have been ten or a dozen people there. Miss Levey herself had already given me several welcoming nods across the room from where she sat, cross-legged and resolutely youthful, on the floor at Evie's feet; and on her black hair was a tissue-paper cap of Liberty, with a red spot on one side of it. I had already discovered that the sounds of nasal singing I had heard came from the metal corolla of a gramophone. This, I surmised, belonged to the gentleman who was operating it, a little Japanese named Kato, whom I had seen once or twice at Aunt Angela's old boarding-house in Woburn Place. He wore a dairymaid's bonnet of pale blue, with torn strings. Two other of Aunt Angela's old fellow-boarders also were there, one of them a delicate little man with white spats, a Mr Trimble, the other an attenuated little lady, with the red marks of a pince-nez across the bridge of her nose, and very thin hair, silver save for a few strands of a yellowish hue. Sitting on Aunt Angela's couch-bed was a younger couple, not very obviously engaged, yet nevertheless carrying on what I gathered to be a courtship by means of quick glad exchanges of the more paradoxical sayings of Schmerveloff. "Oh, rather!" the lady gasped from time to time; "And do you remember that passage?"... "Remember it! *I* should say so—about the 'man-made law' you mean?" These at any rate bore all the marks of being friends of Miss Levey's, and members of the Emancipation Guild. Aunt Angela herself, Evie, and Billy Izzard completed the party.

As I was pushing back my chair, having supped, the gramophone broke out again. Not to interrupt it, I sat where I was, watching the little Japanese who operated it. Mr Kato seemed to have neither eyebrows nor lashes, and the slits of his eyes with their little bitumen dots held, as he looked slyly up from time to time, that indulgent, insulting expression that I distrust in his race over here. He had the appearance of trying the air of the "Intermezzo" from *Cavalleria Rusticana* upon us, as if he contemptuously thought to

The Debit Account

gauge our taste; and his small hands touched screws and lifted little metal arms with a negligent intelligence. He, too, had nodded to me, though our acquaintance was of the slightest; and with him on the one hand, and Miss Levey on the other, I hoped Evie would not want me to stay very long.

The tune had finished, and I had made another motion to rise when suddenly a few words of Miss Levey's caused me to start, and then to sink slowly back into my chair again. She was speaking to Mr Kato.

"Oh, *do* let's have 'Ora pro Nobis' again, Mr Kato—Miss Windus loves it so—don't you, Kitty?"

The next moment the lady whose silver hair was intermixed with brownish strands, the lady whom I had taken to be an old fellow-boarder from Woburn Place, had given a little nod and said "Please." As if to hear the better, she set her pince-nez on her nose.

I saw the little scalene triangles of her eyes....

Like so much obliterating smoke, the past six or seven years rolled away....

Only six or seven years, and I had failed to recognise her!

Not quite knowing what I did, I found myself crossing to the table under the cistern and returning again with a great hacked-off piece of tongue. I sat down to supper again.

There were candles on the table, and little bright refractions of light came darting through the angles of flower-stands and glasses. I watched these as I made pretence to eat. Presently I found myself quite curious about which fleck of light came from which angle, and my eyes sought to trace each sparkle to its origin. A few moments before I had been drinking Burgundy from a green glass; another glass, a red one, stood close to it; but as the candles were placed neither dyed the cloth with the little spot of its own hue. Perhaps—I am trying to tell you quite literally, and as nearly as I can remember, the infantile occupation that had suddenly engrossed me—perhaps if I moved the candle I should get the little spots. I moved the candle this way and that. Presently each of the glasses stood over its own little jewel of light, this one red as a ruby, the other green as grass....

And I cannot better tell you how curiously stunned even my sense of hearing seemed to be than by saying that I heard not one note of "Ora pro Nobis," but only the soft hissing of the cistern overhead in the corner.

But, after I know not what space of time in which I had become half hypnotised by those two tiny refractions of coloured light, I suddenly put the glasses away from me. Also I heard the gramophone once more, and felt the returnings of methodical thought. There came to me, after all this time, the very ordinary reflection that Kitty must have recognised me—had probably known I was coming—and had not been able to endure my presence in the room.... I remembered Evie's words: "I think you are wrong if you think that things like that go on for years and years." Looking covertly up, I saw that Evie had moved, and was now on the other side of Kitty from that occupied by Miss Levey. As I watched, she picked up Kitty's handkerchief, and Kitty smiled. Kitty's eyes even met mine, but whether they saw me or were merely full of "Ora pro Nobis," which was being played for the second or third time, I could not tell. They moved away again without having given any sign of recognition.

Then the tune ended, and Miss Levey jumped up.

"Now, let's have something jolly!" she cried. "And Mr Jeffries has finished his supper—make room for him in the circle—move up, Aschael."

The Debit Account

It came suddenly upon me that there was one place, and one place only in that room for me to take. I had risen. I strode over the box of records in which Mr Kato was rummaging, sat down next to Kitty Windus, and held out my hand.

"How do you do, Kitty?" I said.

So far was she from starting or trembling that she merely turned, blinked a little, and, taking my hand, said, in the thin little voice I used to know so well, "Ah! I *thought* you'd come and speak to me, by-and-by."

So if Miss Levey had deliberately planned this for my confusion, I triumphed over her.

For a quarter of an hour Evie and I sat one on either side of Kitty Windus. There was no difficulty whatever. Kitty, though she spoke little, showed no more restraint than it had been her wont to show, and there was nothing to bring up even the ghost of our past relation. And if I triumphed over Miriam Levey, so Evie triumphed over me in the private glances she gave me past the back of Kitty's head. She had been right, and I wrong. Those stories of how Kitty had been found walking round and round Lincoln's Inn Fields at night, unable, when confronted by a policeman, to remember her own name, or where she lived—I strongly doubted them. I even found Louie's account of her mental state difficult to believe.... She spoke of her neuralgias. She had been a martyr to them, she said, but they had been better lately. Somebody's Tic Mixture had done them more good than anything else. I ought to try it—she'd write the name of it down for me on a piece of paper in case I forgot—she hadn't been remembering things very well lately herself. Louie had advised her to try Somebody Else's Tincture, but she didn't believe in that at all; it was one of these imitations that the shopmen were always trying to palm off on people.... At this point, seeing she had mentioned Louie, I thought it safe to venture an offhand, "Oh, how's Louie, by the way?" But Kitty, apparently forgetting that she herself had introduced the name, pursed her lips. Louie, she mumbled, hadn't behaved very well. She didn't mean to herself; she wouldn't in the least have minded that; but one had friends, and liked to see them treated as friends, which some people—— She stopped as Billy Izzard came up, perhaps hearing Louie's name.

So great was my relief at all this, that I suddenly found myself quite carelessly gay. But for Miss Levey's presence I might have been positively happy. But that lady's fussy attentions to myself did not cause me to drop my guarded attitude towards her. I smiled when she put a paper cap on my head also (she had kept a cracker specially for me, she said); and I made a joke when she read some amatory motto or other; that, I said, would be more in her friends' line—indicating with a glance the couple who conducted the intellectual courtship on the couch. But Miss Levey wagged her short finger at me; she wasn't going to have fun made of the members of her League, she said; and she even went so far as to slap the back of my hand with a paper fan she carried and to tell me I was naughty. Mr Kato, the dotted almonds of his eyes blinkingly comprehending us all, ran through the remaining records and then asked if there were no more; and Aunt Angela herself said that if he wanted more she was afraid he'd have to fetch them from the landing. It was only then that I learned that the gramophone was Aunt Angela's. I had supposed it to belong to Mr Kato.

So we sat and laughed and enjoyed ourselves. Billy Izzard had taken an old letter from his pocket and was making a jotting of the scene. I suppose that mixture of littered supper-table, grotesque tissue-paper caps, and Aunt Angela's miscellaneous furniture must have appealed to his always keen sense of the incongruous. They had got fresh records; I had seen Mr Kato come in with an old soap-box, and had heard Miss Levey's cry of juvenile delight: "Oh, they're all comics!" They were entreating Aschael to sing, who liked being entreated, but said, No, Miriam was the singer. Miriam replied merrily

The Debit Account

that unless they were careful she *would* sing, and then they would know all about it. Aunt Angela laughed heartily at this: and in the end Aschael sang, not very appropriately, "The Boys of the Bulldog Breed." Mr Kato "Hurrahed" and Miss Levey "Banzaied," and Aunt Angela, who had slipped out during the song to wash glasses in her little pantry, called the little nonentity from Woburn Place to help her in giving us all claret-cup.

"What a pity Mr Aschael's voice isn't properly trained!" Kitty remarked, turning to me.

"An awful pity!" Evie struck vivaciously in from the other side of her. "I'm sure he'd have a splendid voice!"

It was odd, the way in which the pair of us took Kitty under our wing.

"You don't sing, do you, Kitty?" Evie next asked.

Kitty didn't. Evie admitted that she didn't either. "But," she said, "we aren't going to let Mr Aschael off with one song, are we? Come, Mr Kato—you're Master of the Ceremonies——"

"I'm just finding one he knows." Mr Kato grinned over his shoulder.

"A comic, mind," warned Miss Levey, "and then Kitty can have 'Ora pro Nobis' again before we go."

And in token that the song was going to be comic, Aschael got up on his feet and set himself in a gesture he had doubtless picked up at the Middlesex Music Hall.

"Now, Mr Aschael," said Kato.

Aschael cleared his throat.

At the first notes of a curiously thin piano accompaniment, I felt Kitty shrink and close as a daisy closes at the approach of night....

You will tell me that I ought to have stopped the machine—smashed it—fallen on it—done something, anything; but put yourself in my place; nay, put yourself in the place of the three of us who sat together, and who had sat together the last time we had heard the song Aschael sang. Did I tell you when that had been, or didn't I? I had better tell you now.... It had been up the River, with a summer twilight falling, and distant banjos sounding, and the Japanese lanterns making long, wavy reflections in the water. Our party had been four, not three, then, and the fourth of us had sung this song Aschael was singing now. He had sung it, lolling in the stern, beating time with one hand, and very careful about the spotting of a new pair of white flannel trousers.

Oh yes, I daresay I ought to have done something rather than let those two other poor things hear *that* song again....

But a hideous fear, of which they knew nothing, kept me fascinated and still. So long as they *only* remembered the song and that other occasion they were the lucky ones. I envied them their luck. No let-off so merciful was mine.... And my horror was enhanced, not so much by those two faces at which I dared not glance, as by our atmosphere of tawdry festivity—the sprinkling of coloured gelatine on the floor, the mocking caps of tissue paper on our heads, and the florid antics of Aschael, turning and grimacing, now this way, now that.

That I might keep this added horror of mine from them, there was even yet a chance....

For the song, you understand, was being sung *twice*, once by the unknown maker of the record in the machine, and the second time, as it were over it, by Aschael. As the two voices did not perfectly coincide, the result was a sort of palimpsest of sound, with, as sometimes happens in palimpsests, the old and almost erased message the more significant one. Aschael kept irregular pace with a far-off amateur voice and the faint tinkling of a piano.... Like a bolt into my brain had come the knowledge of *whose* that horrible instrument had been, and how it had come into Aunt Angela's possession. I remembered her visits to Guildford; I remembered Mrs Merridew's funeral; I remembered her old kindnesses in providing a certain young man in London with a "home from home." The machine had come from Guildford, a legacy, a memento, a giggle from the tomb....

But they, those two poor stricken souls, could yet be spared that knowledge. It was dreadfully too much that they knew the song, and that he had known it, and that he had sung it that summer's evening up the River. The rest of the horror might still be kept from them.

"All together—chorus," cried Aschael jubilantly:

"'Why—don't—you marry the girl?

D'you want—the poor thing—to die?

You can see—she's gone—upon—you

By the twin—kle in—her eye!

Do—the trick—for se—ven-and-six,

Take—the tip—of a pal—

I've—been—watching your game—

Why don't you marry the gal?'"

Then I felt that last desperate hope of mine slipping away—Aschael was beginning to forget the words, and to make out with gestures and grimaces, leaving gaps through which there started up thin and tinkling and facetious horrors.... I saw that Kato had realised; I had once come upon him and Archie drinking whisky and soda together; his eyes met mine curiously, and I fancied his lips shaped the name:

"Merridew?"

This next I have from Billy Izzard. He tells me that all at once I sprang to my feet and cried, in a huge and boisterous voice that drowned everything else, "Never mind, Aschael—chorus—all together!—"

"'Why—don't—you marry the girl?

D'you want—the poor thing to die?

You can see—she's gone—upon you

By the twin-kle in—her eye!

La—la la—sing up!

Take the tip—go on, Aschael!—

I've been—watching your game—

Why don't you marry the gal?'"

Clapping my hands, Billy says, I fell back into a chair.

But I was out of it again in an instant. I was not to escape so easily as all that. Kato had his finger on the lever; I cannot say how, nor whether, he guessed what was to come, nor whether he tried to avert it; if he did, he was too late. From that damnable box there came a long catarrhal wheeze—high-pitched and tenor the words came:

"Now, Evie—Evie's turn—make her sing, mother—bosh—of course she's going to sing!——"

I was neither at Aunt Angela's party nor yet in a boat on a summer's evening up the River. How can I tell you where I was? In what drawing-room? Sitting on what chair?

Surrounded by what company?... I swear to you that I have seen a place I have never seen, been in a place I never in my life was in. I can describe to you a family gathering with Mrs Merridew there, and her son there, and Evie there, and myself never, never there. I have seen, whether they ever existed or not, French windows opening on a lawn, and a slackened tennis-net beyond, and an evening flush in the sky, and the air dark with homing rooks.... Nothing will persuade me that these eyes are in fact ignorant of that quiet home of Archie Merridew's—and yet Guildford is a place in which I have never been.

Then a sound like the hissing of a thousand cisterns filled my ears. Through it I heard Kitty Windus's scream of terror, but it sounded an infinite distance away. From Evie I had heard nothing. For one moment I saw everything reel and aslant—Kato, the Schmerveloffians on the sofa, the cistern-post with its hats and coats and one hook empty, steeving up towards a tilted ceiling....

Then came the blow on the back of my head, and the sounds of the cistern ceased. I had fallen across Aunt Angela's tiled hearth, and lay in a cloud of steam from the kettle I had overturned in my fall.

PART IV IDDESLEIGH GATE

I

It is against the advice of my doctors that I have written these last pages—these last chapters in fact—at all. But I wrote them only a very little at a time, after I came back from Hastie's place in Scotland. And I went to Scotland only after I came back from Egypt. But I am back at the Consolidation now, having missed nearly a year, and I really don't think that this private writing tires me too much.

I admit that it seems odd that I should wish to do it at all, and doubly odd that I should have kept, not one private record, but two. I thought I had finished when the first one came to an end. Then I found I hadn't. Let me say quite plainly, however, that the second one is no retractation of the first. There is not a single statement in that first writing from which I recede. I stand by every word of it. I wrote there, for example, that I did not fear to be left alone in my library at night; and that is true. I wrote that there glided no shadowy shape by my side when I stepped into my brougham or passed between the saluting commissionaires in Pall Mall; and that also is true. It is true that I play with my clean-born children, both of them, and still do not pardon even the meditation of that old crime that would have made the life of her I love an abhorrence worse than death. These things are as true now as when I first wrote them, and I shall die without regret for them.

But the impulse that drives a man to write about himself at all still remains a curious thing. I don't find it an inexplicable one—but as I shall return to this by-and-by, I will leave it for the present. Let me say this, however, now; that whatever cares may or may not weigh on me, I neither consider myself on my defence nor yet join hands with Schmerveloff and his crew in their sweeping and futile denunciations of the whole Scheme of Things as they are. If I cannot stand alone I can at least fall alone, and I haven't fallen yet.

Nevertheless, this writing will have to be less frequently indulged (if that is the word); there is little sense in paying doctors if you don't take their advice. There have been few physically stronger men than I; especially my strength of finger and forearm and wrist have been remarkable; and I can still bend a half-crown and make a dog's leg out of a thick poker. But I don't pretend that I am the man I was. Separately, my brain and body work as well as ever they did, but they do not always jump together. I don't know whether this is due to the hole Aunt Angela's blackleaded fender made in my skull. It was a bad hole, and I cracked three of Aunt Angela's brown tiles. Perhaps that is the reason why my doctor advised me to get to bed early, and cautioned me about the use of stimulating drinks and heating foods.... Let me see, let me see....

Ah, yes, I was going to speak of that evening. Mercifully, Evie was spared the worst of that shock. So gently and easily that for quite a time nobody discovered it, she had slid off into a faint at the very beginning of that song of Aschael's, and so had not seen my own headlong fall. This saved us from a disaster, for otherwise our little girl would probably not have been born in the following July, not to be welcomed by her father until October came. Indeed, I had to wait till October before I learned a good many things; but such was my state of lassitude that I was able to do so without impatience, and even without much interest, content to be free from pain and to be looked after by those people of Hastie's party. After a time they began to allow me to do little things—superintend the packing of the luncheon-baskets and, as I grew better, to join the guns in the clearing when the whistle went; and Evie, away at Broadstairs with Aunt Angela (who had given up her room in the little "circus"), sometimes seemed part of a charming but not very moving dream to me. You see from this how bad I was.... Then I returned, and the winter in Egypt and Hastie's house in Scotland began in their turn to fade.

Apart from my work at the Consolidation, I began to be full of a curiously single preoccupation. I had not brooded on this while I had been away: as I have said, I had not brooded on anything; it merely came back to me as the most natural thing to do, a matter of course. It was the thing that Louie Causton, against what she conceived to be her own interests, had advised that night when I had dined with her at the Models' Club. There was something I must now tell Evie.

I think I let it go, vaguely, as "something." It was not that I did not know perfectly well what it was; but those lazy days free from pain among the heather had made that also somehow unreal; I suppose I had worn smooth the thought of it; and it seemed nothing to make a fuss about. It did not even require resolution. It was merely something that ought to have been done long ago. This was my attitude of mind then. I don't say that it is now.

That long separation had altered our relation in more ways than one. With such joy did I rejoin Evie that for both of us it was as if we were newly, and yet both more strongly and more peacefully, married again. My lovely little Phyllis had put even poor Jackie's nose out of joint. On the other hand, a year is a year, and if my own time had been one of vacancy and healing, Evie's had not. I had only to listen to her and Aunt Angela to become aware of this. They had made quite a circle of acquaintances in Broadstairs; several of these had since been kept up in London; and there were things I was at least temporarily out of. I mention this not because I wanted to be in at them; indeed it all seemed to me a little casual; but I could hardly have expected Evie to sit moping in a boarding-house parlour all that time, and certainly she looked a picture of blooming health. I say "looked," because it was only later that I learned what the first question of the doctor who had attended her had been: "Has she ever had a severe shock?"

The Debit Account

I am unable to explain how it was that at first I was quite incurious to know what people had thought of that extraordinary collapse of mine, and why the effect of that song on Kitty Windus, for example, should have been less marked than its effect on myself. For Kitty, though she had screamed, and babbled incoherent things that probably I have never been told about, had sustained no lasting injury. An icy breath had passed over everybody there, and nobody, I thought, would be so morbid as to push their inquiries into the varying degrees of iciness. I may say at once that I thought quite rightly. Nobody has, not even (so far as I am aware) Miriam Levey.

It was from Aunt Angela, of course, that I learned what that first question of the Broadstairs doctor had been; and it brought me face to face with that so easily assumed resolution of mine rather sharply. By mere luck Evie had escaped that shock of the party, but the original one, the seven or eight years' old one, remained. That I might know exactly to what extent this might affect my determination, I had the Broadstairs doctor to meet my own more distinguished one. I told this one of the tragedy of Evie's former engagement, and related the affair of the gramophone. He looked grave.

"You must see that she doesn't get another shock," he said.

Evie herself was not made aware that the visit had more than an ordinary significance.

But Louie's advice now seemed rather beside the mark.

I saw Louie daily now; and whether it was that she had been able to entrench herself behind her work in my absence, or had found some *modus vivendi* midway between that ecstasy of the night when she had supported me in a Chelsea doorway and the anguished outbreak of that other evening in the Models' Club, or however it was, my fears for the impossibility of the situation now appeared to have been groundless. Whitlock, indeed, saw more of her than I. He spoke exceedingly favourably of her. She used quickness and common-sense in her work, he said, and, when he had half-a-dozen things to do at once, did not take down a remark interpolated to somebody else as part of the letter he was dictating. I was not surprised to learn that she "flashed" intelligently at unexplained meanings. She converted Whitlock's rapid mumbled instructions into (commercial) English with ease, and had already attracted Pepper's notice.

I don't know whether it has struck you that Evie, who had given it as a sufficient reason for renewing her intimacy with Miriam Levey and Kitty Windus that they had been at the old Business College in Holborn together, had never once urged the same thing on behalf of Louie Causton. It was not that I wanted her to do so; as a matter of fact I very much preferred them apart. And I thought I saw the reason for Evie's silence. Louie trailed an unhappy story behind her. Louie had been a model. Aunt Angela had not asked her to her party. If there was any coolness between Miriam Levey and Louie, which now might well be, Evie would naturally be disposed to take the part of the former. I don't mean to say that she looked down on Louie. It was only later that I learned that she wasted a thought on Louie. I only mean that their paths lay in different directions, and that Evie had hitherto appeared content that they should do so.

It was in a roundabout way that I discovered that Louie had a place in Evie's thoughts. Acting under my doctor's orders, I had begun to come home early in the afternoon, seldom working after tea; and I entered the drawing-room one afternoon to find a couple of her Broadstairs acquaintances, a Mr and Mrs Smithson, with her. Smithson was, I think, a cycle agent; she was an openwork-stockinged, flirtatious little woman, for ever making eyes, and apparently under the impression that all conversation would languish unless she took the greater part of it upon herself. I imagine it had been she who had sent Evie one or two vulgar seaside post cards that, had they been addressed to me, would have gone straight into the fire. It appeared that they knew Peddie slightly, my old Jun.

The Debit Account

Ex. Con. of the F.B.C., and now Whitlock's abstract clerk; and I was not disposed to congratulate Peddie on the acquaintance.

They were just leaving as I arrived, so that we only exchanged a few words; indeed, the ringing of the telephone I had had fixed up in my study gave me an excuse to cut our leave-taking short. I went to the instrument; it was Louie Causton with a message from Whitlock; and I gave my instructions and returned to Evie.

Now Jackie, who was just beginning to babble and notice things, was greatly interested in the telephone, and I entered the drawing-room just in time to hear him make some remark about "plitty typies." As I took no notice, Jackie repeated the unchildlike expression. Evie was pouring me out more tea.

"Plitty typies, farzer," Jackie clamoured, imperious for notice.

I turned to Evie.

"Where did he pick that up?" I asked.

Evie said: "Oh, it was some silly joke of Florrie's."

"Florrie is Mrs Smithson?"

"Yes."

I was not pleased. I suppose that, like Charles Lamb, I am squeamish about my women and children, and I remembered Mrs Smithson's post cards. One of them had borne the legend, "Detained at office—very pressing business," and if you have seen these things you will not want it described. But I was loth to raise again the question I had formerly raised about Miss Levey and Aschael, and so I merely asked whether it was not possible for her to give Mrs Smithson tea without having Jackie there. She said, "Very well," though in a tone a little subdued. She knew what I meant.

It was ten minutes later that, returning of her own accord to the subject, she said a little poutingly: "I don't see much to make a fuss about. He doesn't know what it means."

"That doesn't improve matters very much," I said. "It seems to me to make them worse."

"Oh, very well," she answered.

But she returned to the subject yet again. She spoke defensively.

"I had to have him at Broadstairs with me. You couldn't have him in Scotland with you."

"Jackie, you mean?"

"Yes."

She gave a slightly marked shade of meaning to the words "in Scotland." To tell the truth, it was a little on my mind that I had had the more desirable summer of the two of us. I am no snob, but I do prefer some people to others, and if people do run in strata, well, nobody can tell me much I don't know about the clerk and cycle-agent class, and they don't charm me. I spoke with a little compunction.

"I wish it could have been helped, darling. Anyway, we sha'n't be separated again."

(I may say that I don't think Evie had thought it very remarkable that I should have had that accident at Aunt Angela's party. She had fainted herself, and knew little of the later events; and we have lived too long together for her not to be aware that, rugged as I may appear to the rest of the world, I am a sensitive man.)

After a moment's silence: "Mrs Smithson has asked me down to Broadstairs for a week," she said. "She—of course she hadn't met you."

"You mean she's asked you without me?"

The Debit Account

"She hadn't met you," Evie excused Mrs Smithson.

"And—shall you go?"

She answered quite readily: "Of course not—not without you."

I got up and kissed her. I had expected no less of her.

But I knew that she would have liked to go to Broadstairs, and was only staying away out of her duty to me, it was not for me to deny her her sex's equivalent of a grumble—a sigh. Then we began to talk.

We talked quite equably: I never in my life wrangled with Evie. I said, quite gently, that I did not wish the boy to acquire precocious chatter about pressing business and pretty typists, and Evie made no opposition; indeed, she laughed when I suggested how unlikely it was that any pretty typist would have pressing business with myself. By-and-by she asked me who had rung me up, and I told her. "Oh, yes, I forgot; she's with you now," she said; "Mr Whitlock engaged her, didn't he?"

"Yes," I answered. Then, after a little further talk, we kissed again, and she went out to give Phyllis her bath.

Oddly enough, very soon after speaking thus of Louie after that long silence, she saw Louie herself. One morning she announced that she was going shopping that day, and would call for me at Pall Mall and bring me home to tea. She finished her shopping earlier than she had thought she would, and, not wishing to disturb me before the appointed time, had come upon Louie in the counting-house. She told me this when we got home. She had asked Louie to show her round, and was full of the wonders of the place—the lifts, the telephone exchange, the series of waiting-rooms, the advice-board from Lloyd's, the acre-wide office full of busy clerks. "What a change from Holborn!" she said she had said to Louie, and then Louie had brought her to my own private room.

The next day Louie made a mistake in a rather important draft. It was not like her, and Whitlock blamed himself for having left too much to her intuition. The error necessitated a consultation between Louie, Whitlock and myself. It was set right, and Louie was going out again when I glanced at Whitlock. He looked inquiringly, nodded, and left us. There was something I wanted to say to Louie; perhaps it was rather something that it would not be very graceful not to say; perhaps it was both.

I think this was the first time I spoke to her at the Consolidation except on business.

"Well, that will be all right," I said, dismissing the error in the draft.... "By the way, you saw my wife yesterday, didn't you?"

She gave a little nod.

"And showed her round? It was very good of you. She enjoyed it very much. She told me all about it."

Louie said something about it being no trouble, and then appeared to be going. But I stopped her. Then, when I had stopped her, I didn't quite know what to say.

"Oh—er——" I said awkwardly, looking at her and then looking away again. "Without opening matters up—you know what I mean—going into things—I want to say just one thing. It's about—a piece of advice you once gave me."

She had half opened the inner door, and stood, as it were, on the threshold of the box-like space between the inner one and the outer one of baize. The look she gave me was almost hostile, and the tourmalines were shut. I don't think, by the way, that she ever heard of that incident at Aunt Angela's party. I neither asked her whether she had, nor ever told her about it.

"If you feel that you must——" she said, not very invitingly.

"It's merely this," I said rather hurriedly, "that what you suggested is impossible now."

"Yes," she said; "I suppose it is."

"Her doctor's forbidden it—I mean, he says she mustn't have another shock."

Instantly I saw, by the way in which she said, "Oh!" that she had had something else in her mind. "Oh!... I see," she said, and I pondered.

"Ah!" I said at last. "You mean you've just seen—just this moment?"

She made no reply.

"You've just seen, just this moment. Then why did you say yes, you supposed so?"

Her answer was impatient. "Oh, *must* you?"

"Must I what?"

"Must you do this?"

"Ask you why you assented when I said something was impossible now?"

"Ask me anything at all!" she almost snapped.

I gave her a long look. "Shut the door," I said.... "Now tell me why you agreed with me when I said that it was impossible to take your advice now."

The tourmalines flickered almost scornfully. "Don't you know?"

"I do not."

"What! You can't guess?"

"Will you tell me?"

For a moment she looked as if she was going to sit down for something that would require time; but she changed her mind, and stood, a crumple of skirt grasped in either hand.

"Ask me again and I will," she said, in a slightly raised voice.

"I do ask you."

Then, with a harsh little laugh, Louie made her second mistake of that day.

"Because she's jealous," she said. "Evidently that wasn't *your* reason; I don't know what yours was; but that's mine."

"Oh!" I said. In the face of a statement so preposterous I really could think of nothing else to say.

"What else did she come here yesterday for?" Louie demanded.

I smiled. That was too absurd. "Well—shall we say to keep an appointment with her husband?" I suggested.

"Oh, if you like!... Then why does she want to come and see me at my house?" she demanded.

It was news to me that Evie did want to go and see Louie at her house, but I was careful not to let Louie see that.

"Oh!" I said, still smiling. "And you think these grounds enough for your statement?"

"My good——" she broke out. "I'm not asking you to accept them. I know better than to try to persuade *you*! You asked me, and I've told you; that's all."

"And if I say once for all that it is not so, and that nothing could make it so?"

"Make it so!" she broke out. "Really, Jeff, you talk like—a man! 'Make it so!'... If you can't see your little definite reason for everything, you deny the fact! If I could say that Kitty Windus and Miriam Levey had been chattering—I'm not aware that they have, but if I *could* say that—I suppose you'd call that a reason, and listen to it; but anything else—pshaw! I don't care a button for your reason! Your reason may have made this business, but it won't persuade a woman against something she knows—myself *or* Evie. It just is so, and there's an end of it. And of course you see the beautiful new fix it puts you in." She gave a little stamp that made her garments quiver.

"Louie, I can't——"

"Oh, a perfect fix! Really, I'm curious to know what you're going to do about it! Try to persuade her that there's nothing between you and me! Try it, try it! Why, how shouldn't she be jealous when I am? Do you think she doesn't see that? Oh, I don't know why I waste words with you!... But you see your fix. It was Kitty before, and you tried half telling then; now it's me; but it isn't either of us really; oh, if it only could be!... It's the secret, Jim. You've got to tell her—and you can't. I don't know what this is about a shock, but it's too late now. Try it if you like—I don't care what you say about me. Try the half truth again—give her reason—the reason's yours whenever you want it."

Of course I couldn't listen to this nonsense and immodesty and worse. Who should know better whether Evie was jealous or not, Louie or I? Evie jealous!... Of course, if it were so, the position *would* be precisely as Louie had stated it. I *should* have to choose between Evie's love and the risk the doctor had so gravely foreshadowed. Our very existence together *would* hang on precisely that last desperate chance. And from the bottom of my heart I blessed my Maker that, tossed and buffeted as my life had been, at least that perfected anguish of body and spirit was to be spared me....

I had risen. Smiling rather sadly, I turned to Louie.

"Well—as I said—I don't want to re-open things," I said.

With the door already half open, she turned.

"Do you think they're closed?" she said.

And she did not wait for my reply.

FOOTNOTE:
See "In Accordance with the Evidence."

II

It is as I feared: this writing, as a continuous record, will have to stop. My life is getting too full. I daresay its crowded outward happenings are a good thing for me; it is better, as the saying is, to wear out than to rust out; and I am beginning almost to enjoy change for change's sake.

My newest change is a removal. Pepper's latest cosmopolitan, Baron Stillhausen, wants to be rid of that Iddesleigh Gate house as it stands, and already I have taken Evie round to see it. It almost took away her breath: I didn't know how near delight could come to timidity—I almost said to dismay. When I said, "Well, darling, am I to take it?" she looked at me as much as to say "*Dare* you?"... I think I dare—though I have only to remember my own beginnings to be a little intimidated myself. I walked over to Verandah Cottage the other evening; a sign-writer has the place now; and it seems either very much more or very much less than four years since I lived there—sometimes hardly four months, sometimes half-a-lifetime.... But Evie will very quickly be turning up her nose at Well Walk. Already she had begun to shop quite freely. For getting to and from Pall Mall (I told you I was to spare myself physically for the present) I have bought a small runabout of a car. Really it is only an ordinary taxi, with a rather superior shell placed on it, and I have an agreement with a young fellow who has just taken his driving certificate; but Evie was talking about a livery for him the other night, and I was pleased. That is as it should be. It will be a joy to me to see her take her proper place....

So this record will have to be more and more a diary, jotted down as I can find opportunity for it. I need not say that the change to Iddesleigh Gate will be a larger undertaking than, say, Aunt Angela's installation in the little "circus" near King's Cross was. And there is the Consolidation. That is heavy work, and the heavier that at present we are working very much in the dark. In these present industrial troubles, for example, we do not quite know where we shall come out; we can only throw in our weight with the big natural forces that, in history as in dynamics, balance themselves in the end. The air is thick with dust of Schmerveloff's raising; and though all this dust may turn out presently to be like the comet's tail, packable into a portmanteau, for the present it certainly obscures our vision. We have to take into account, too, that even dust is not raised without a cause; and so in public we sit, Radicals all, in solemn inquiry into things, with plenty of Westminster stage thunder, while behind the scenes we get in good old Tory heavy work, not necessarily because we are Tories, but because Toryism serves a useful purpose just at present. Once or twice lately I have disobeyed my doctor, and stayed at the office for tea, so closely in touch have I had to keep with various Committees and Conferences; and we have had to keep our staff late too, which is rather hard on them, since they get none of the kudos. But the days when I could burn the candle at both ends all the time are over for me, I'm afraid.

Louie Causton rarely gets away early now; in that respect she was better off when she sat for the evening classes at the Art Schools; but she gravitates more and more to Pepper's side of the business. That bee she has in her bonnet about Evie's being jealous of her does not, I am glad to say, impair her business efficiency. The other day Pepper remarked on her distinguished carriage, and, as he never neglects appearances, he chooses her, when an amanuensis is necessary, for his more important consultations. The other night he took her and Whitlock to dinner before going to Sir Peregrine Campbell's. I can picture his dismay had it ever been suggested that he should take Miss Levey out to dinner. And Stonor and Peddie do not crack the old jokes they did at the F.B.C., about "Miss Causton's pal—Sir Peregrine," or "You know who I mean—that friend of Miss Causton's—the Under Secretary for Foreign Affairs." Indeed there seem to be fewer jokes going about than there used to be. We are all getting older—Louie (save for those slender yacht-like lines of hers), Aunt Angela (whose self-satisfied humilities have rather lost their resilience since that night of her housewarming in the little "circus"), Evie (who now takes the prospect of a day and a night nursery as a matter of course, and has bills sent in to me quite naturally) and the rest of us. Even Billy Izzard, clean painter as he is, seems to be forcing his jokes. He has lately found an artificial amusement in balls and pageants, rather to the neglect of his work; and all this, slight as it seems—I mean the spread of the love of amusement—has actually more to do with Consolidation than you would guess.... But I must stop. I get Consolidation enough during the day without bringing it home with me at night. Evie has just knocked at the door. That is her signal that I have "consolidated" enough—as she calls this journal of which she has never heard.

1st March.—For the first time I make this frankly a diary. According to my agreement, we go into Iddesleigh Gate on Lady Day; as a matter of fact we are there now. My lease is for ten years. I got as many of Stillhausen's effects as I wanted at forced-sale rates; a good deal I didn't want. Evie went half wild with joy about a certain crystal bath; I about

The Debit Account

the Amaranth Room. It is extraordinary how few pieces it takes to furnish this last splendid apartment: a settee, a few chairs, a few cabinets, a bust or two, and the vast turfy carpet.... A smaller room would look half empty with twice the furniture. Billy says it's the proportions, and is puzzling about them, seeking what he calls "the unit," and taking now the length of a gilt Empire settee, now the height of a lacquered cabinet, now his own height, etc., etc. It is Evie's music room; she has begun her lessons; but it will be some time, I am afraid, before she makes very much of it. Billy threatens to quarter himself on us while he makes paintings of the whole house. Aunt Angela has two rooms on the second floor, with distempered walls; and she began her furnishing with a crucifix. My library is stately. The heavy, slow-moving doors scarcely make a click when they close, and a bell-connection down the passage warns me of the approach of anybody. I suppose Stillhausen found this useful; he was in the Diplomatic Service; and perhaps it is well that these stamped leather walls do not whisper secrets. There is a secret of my own that I keep in the bureau by the heat-regulator there. I am not sure that the fire would not be the best place for it. It is odd, by the way, that this impulse to burn these papers should lately have become almost as strong as the impulse to write them formerly was.

I have a telephone switchboard to half the rooms in the house, and the line to Pall Mall is doubled, the second wire not passing through the Company's Exchange. A switch turns on the masked lights behind the cornice, and what with one device and another, it would pay me to have a private electrician. Aunt Angela, I may say, who has managed to reconcile herself to heavier expenditures, is harrowed at the waste of electric power, and wanders about the house turning off switches. On a Jacobean table at the far end of the library are two small bright things with branches—that is to say, they seem small until you take a walk to them. They are Pepper's candlesticks. I have attained the scale.

28th March.—That impulse to destroy these papers has reminded me of a little thing that happened while I was away in Scotland. One of Hastie's boys, Ronald, aged fourteen, has a little den of his own in the back part of the house, and during my convalescence he was so good as to make me welcome there. The paraphernalia of I don't know how many hobbies littered the place; his latest had been chemistry; and he stank of chemicals, and had his clothes red-spotted with acids. His greatest success, at which I was privileged to assist, was to fill ginger-beer bottles with hydrogen and explode them. One day he invited me to witness a really superior explosion. It was lucky he did invite me. He had charged an earthenware jar, as big as a bucket, with the gas and would probably have blown the wall out. He said he didn't funk it, but I did, and we opened the window and allowed the gas to be lost.

I feel rather like that about this writing. Last night I almost made away with the dangerous stuff. But I hung back. It has cost so hideously dear. This may be a sentimentalism, and obscure, but there it is, and as it puzzles me I shall try to get to the bottom of it....

N.B.—Evie says she will soon "begin to feel that she lives here." She is getting used to having things; soon she will be getting used to having people. Soon she'll have to be thinking about her first dinner-party. Must stop now. The more sleep I get before midnight the better. I shall think about the destroying, though.

29th April.—(A month since I made an entry.) A rather curious conversation with Evie last night. You will remember that Louie Causton, trying to justify that ridiculous attitude of hers about Evie's jealousy, had exclaimed, as if that clinched something, "Why does she want to come to my house, then?" Well, she has been. Apparently she went some little time ago, but she only spoke of it last night. I shall not ask Louie for her account of it; this is Evie's:

She went on a Saturday afternoon, taking the train from Clapham Junction. Louie was just setting out with her boy to the South Kensington Museum, but she turned back. Since Kitty left her she has got another governess for the lad, but she still devotes her Saturdays and Sundays to him. There are several things about Evie's account I am not quite clear about, but I admit that she has no great gift for picking out the essentials of a conversation, and perhaps unconsciously she has emphasised the wrong things. She told me, for example, a good deal about Master Jim, but said very little about Kitty's reason for going over to Miriam Levey. She wandered off into old recollections of the Business College in Holborn that I had forgotten all about, and allowed these things to divert her from the visit itself. I had to ask her whether Louie seemed comfortable in her rooms, whether they were decently furnished or not, and so on; and she said, "Oh, of course, you've never seen them," and described them to me in excellent detail. Then suddenly she asked me whether Miss Lingard (who had been away out of sorts), was back at the Consolidation yet. Miss Lingard was my own private amanuensis, and during her absence Louie had had to help with her work.... And so we talked. This was in our own bedroom, while Evie was making ready for the night.

"Well," I said, yawning, "and what did you talk about besides the Holborn days?"

"Oh, lots of things," she answered brightly, busily brushing. "She's got to look older since then—but I daresay you wouldn't notice that, seeing her every day."

"Louie Causton, you mean?"

"Yes."

"Did she say anything about Miss Levey?"

"Oh, yes. Her correspondence class is a great success. Schmerveloff's taken her up, and she's no end of pupils. Wasn't it funny, our living next door to Schmerveloff and not knowing it? They little thought that in a few years we should be living here!"

I laughed a little. She glows prettily when she shows her pride in my achievement. Then I yawned again. "Well," I said sleepily, "I hope Kitty's changed friends for the better."

"Oh, she thinks so," Evie replied promptly. "You see, it wasn't very nice for her, when she'd had the boy all days, and Louie didn't come in till ten or eleven or twelve at night, or later, to be snapped at and spoken crossly to."

Here I checked a yawn. "What's that?" I said. "Miss Causton didn't tell you that, did she?"

"Eh?" said Evie. "Oh, no, of course she didn't. Didn't I tell you I looked in at their offices in Gray's Inn one day—Kitty's and Miriam's? Oh, that was a fortnight and more ago! I'm sure I told you, Jeff!... And Miriam took me to the New College in Kingsway. It's nothing like the Consolidation, of course, but it's such an improvement on that poky old Holborn place! How we ever gave a dance there I can't imagine. You remember that dance, Jeff?"

And she was back at the old College once more.

I said this conversation was curious, but perhaps that was not quite the word. Slightly distasteful would be nearer, for of course you see what it all implied. It implied that Evie might easily be dragged into some trumpery quarrel between Louie Causton and Miriam Levey. For Miriam would not be at all above concluding that Louie had schemed to get her place, and that I had thrown my influence into the balance; and anybody could always make poor Kitty agree with them. I didn't want Evie mixed up in anything of that kind. I was even a little sorry she had been to see Louie. How little, for my own part, there existed in the way of affection between Louie and myself you already know; and, if the thing was not quite the same from Louie's point of view, I did not see that any useful end would be served by their being much together. On that morning when Louie had first made her ridiculous suggestion about jealousy, her whole manner had been rather that of one who throws up the sponge, ceases to exercise care, I don't know what; and there is no sense in deliberately manufacturing something that doesn't exist. And about that other visit to Gray's Inn. I am quite sure that Miriam Levey would not scruple to hurt me in any way she could.... There's the telephone; Whitlock, I expect.

10th May.—In a week Evie is to give her first dinner-party. Naturally she is a little timorous about it. The fact that Pepper, with whom, I am sorry to say, she gets on no better, will be there to watch her, would be quite enough to flurry her; but there will also be other people there whom she hasn't seen yet—the Hasties, the Campbells, Sichel, a Mrs Richmond (a very smart little woman, a friend of Pepper's) and others. Poor dear, it will be rather an ordeal for her, and no wonder she spoke to me the other night a little crossly. It hurt a little at the time, but I have forgotten it. I will put it down, however.

Among all these "Hons. and Sirs," as she calls them, plain familiar Whitlock and Billy Izzard (I am dragging Billy in because these people may be useful to him when he has got over his pageant craze) were her chief comforts; but the question of the final chair, a lady's, had arisen. There being nobody else I particularly wanted, I had been disposed to call on Pepper, who can always produce a prettily frocked woman or a well-turned-out young man at a moment's notice; but Evie had managed to get a dig in at Pepper, at which I laughed heartily. "He might bring Mrs Toothill for all we know," she had said. "No, Jeff, it's our party," she had demurred, and had then ruminated....

"All right, anybody you like," I had agreed cheerfully.

"You don't like Mrs Smithson," she had then said doubtfully.

Of course, having just given her full liberty, I ought not to have qualified it, even by a look; but I confess my face fell. It was only for an instant, and I hoped my darling hadn't noticed it.

"Have Mrs Smithson if you like," I said a little shortly, I am afraid.

But she had noticed. She spoke shortly too.

"No, thank you, not to have her thrown in my face afterwards. I know you don't think the Smithsons are good enough."

I was shocked. "Dearest," I said slowly, "when have I 'thrown things in your face afterwards,' as you call it?"

She must indeed have been tried, otherwise she would never have said the absurd thing she did.

"Well, if you don't say it, you think it. Better have your friend, Miss Causton. She can go out to dinner with Sir Julius, it seems."

"Evie!" I exclaimed, for the moment deeply wounded.

"Well, you told me she did, and if she can dine with him she can with you, I suppose."

I turned away. "I shall leave it entirely to you," I said. I reproach myself now for my impatience.

But instantly her generous little heart was itself again. She ran after me and threw her arms about my neck.

The Debit Account

"Forgive me, Jeff," she pleaded tearfully. "I didn't mean anything, and I am *so* afraid of it all! I'm *not* used to it, you know, but I am doing my best. Do ask Mr Pepper to bring somebody."

And we kissed and said no more about it. Perhaps I am foolish to write it down.

14th May.—Evie has made the acquaintance of most of her guests for the seventeenth beforehand. The Hasties have called on her, and Lady Campbell, and Pepper has brought Mrs Richmond (who, I confess, strikes me as rather a superfine Mrs Smithson), and half her fears are gone. She didn't much care for Mrs Richmond, she says; "toney" was the adjective she used; but she quite took dear homely Lady Campbell under her wing. She likes receiving, she says, and remarked, rather acutely, that what makes these little afternoon functions the occasion for bickering they are, is that people seem to rattle off what they have to say without an interval for breath, and then to take their departure. She had Jackie down, and Phyllis was brought down for a moment by her nurse; and Jackie showed Lady Campbell his ship. Lady Campbell married her husband when he was master and a fifth-part owner of a coasting boat; and when Jackie lifted the hatch of his model to show her the "cabin" she laughed, and said it was a far more comfortable cabin than that in which she spent her honeymoon. Then Jackie, of course, wanted to know what a honeymoon was, and when told made some remark about a honeymoon that set everybody laughing except Evie, who blushed. I hope she will not forget how to blush among all her smart ladies. I find her blushing adorable.

17th May, 4 P.M.—Without warning, a thing that I had thought impossible has come upon me. For nearly twenty hours—since nine o'clock last night—my thoughts have been such a series of jerks, stoppings, leapings forward and dead stops again as only once before in my life I have known. I have paced my private room at the Consolidation for half the day, and have done no work since I looked over and signed the papers that were brought to me here last night. Were I able to speak of "mere nothings" I should say that a mere nothing has brought all this about. Let me tell it. I have come home for the purpose of telling it.

Since I began to leave the Consolidation early, papers have often been brought to me here. Usually Stonor brings them, and is shown straight into the library. You may judge of their urgency when I tell you that last night there was nobody to bring them but Louie Causton.

Evie, Aunt Angela and I were just finishing dinner when the servant whispered to me. I think he said "Somebody from Pall Mall, sir," for if he had said "A lady" I should have wondered who the lady was, which I didn't do. I was expecting the papers; they would not keep me long; so, telling Evie that I should be back in a few minutes, I followed the servant out.

Louie was standing by my desk. She had not lifted her veil, and I do not know what it was about her attitude that struck me. Something did; I suppose it was some proportion or relation; something that Billy would perhaps have called the "beautiful unit" of the room; some purely æsthetic quality, I don't doubt, which it is odd I should remember now.... She was looking towards me as I entered; she had heard that discreet bell of Stillhausen's; and only when I advanced did she push her veil back.

"Here are these," she said, with a twisted, pained sort of little smile. "The others had all gone home, and I understood they were to come at once. No, thanks, I won't sit down."

Even when it appeared that, after all, the papers would need a few minutes' looking into, she still refused to sit down. She stood as close to the papers she had brought as if,

The Debit Account

without them, her sole reason for being there, she might have been ejected; and as she still persisted in her refusal to sit, I sat down myself.

It took me perhaps a quarter of an hour to go through the papers. It was as I was pushing back my chair that Stillhausen's bell purred again. A moment later there was a tap at the door. "Come in!" I called.

Evie entered.

I was not embarrassed. It humiliates me to have to write that word now, so many hours later. There was nothing to be embarrassed at. Indeed, as Evie advanced from the door, I barely explained the reason for Miss Causton's call. Louie touched the hand Evie extended. Evie was not, as she was with Miriam Levey and Kitty Windus, on kissing terms with Louie.

"I think you'll find these all right now," I said, giving Louie back the papers. "I don't know whether Miss Causton has had supper, Evie?"

Evie smiled graciously. "Yes, won't you have something, Miss Causton? Let me have them lay a tray for you—it will be really no trouble."

But Louie would take nothing. She had drawn down her veil again, and was extending her fingers to Evie. "Don't trouble to come, Mr Jeffries," she said, moving towards the door, while Evie prattled polite phrases.

But I took her to the door. Four words—a "Good-night" on either side—were all that passed between us. Then I returned to the library.

Evie was standing where Louie had been standing, but no sooner did I enter than she passed me. Taking into account the warning of Stillhausen's bell, she must have waited for the purpose of so passing me. But this did not strike me until a little later. Only when she reached the door did she turn and speak.

"Did Miss Causton ask for me?" she said.

"Eh?" I asked, surprised.... "No. Why?"

"Oh, nothing. Only that I thought that when one called one asked for the lady of the house."

I smiled as I set my writing-table to rights. "'Called?' It was hardly a call, my dear."

"Evidently not."

I looked quickly up. Evie's tone was new to me.

"Come, come, darling—a necessary matter of business," I expostulated.

"I'm sorry I interrupted."

"'Interrupted!'... Good gracious, Evie!"

"But of course I didn't; you can't be interrupted here."

I was astonished.

"Why, what—what do you mean?"

She looked coldly at me, without replying.

I frowned. I am ashamed to say that it cost me a little effort to master an impatience that had suddenly arisen in me. I spoke slowly for that purpose.

"If by your last remark you mean that bell, Evie, it was here before we came, and I fancy you knew it was. At any rate it shall be taken away to-morrow."

Very irritatingly (I have told you how I am not quite the man of phlegm I was) she took me up at my last word.

"Oh, yes, about to-morrow," she said. "You don't happen to be going out to-night, do you?"

"No. Why?" This was stranger than ever. She knew I never went out at night now.

"Because Mrs. Hastie telephoned me to-day. Joan isn't well, and can't come. So perhaps you'd like Sir Julius to ask somebody else—unless, of course——"

"Unless what?"

"Unless—there's somebody you'd rather ask yourself."

For a moment I was silent; then, "Evie," I said slowly, "do you—I don't see how you can, but do you—mean Louie Causton?"

She laughed tremulously. "Oh, very well; if I can't, I can't, I suppose, so that ends it."

And the next moment she was gone.

Half-an-hour later I met her on the stairs.

"Oh," she announced, without preface, "Phyllis isn't very well, and I think I shall spend the night in the nursery with her."

She has done so.

I have had a wretched night. I turned and turned, but found no sleep. By dint of turning, I found something else, though—a new meaning in those words Louie Causton had said to me: "If I could say that Miriam Levey and Kitty Windus had been chattering, which I can't——" I tossed and tossed.

At half-past ten this morning I went round to the offices of the Women's Emancipation League in Gray's Inn. I can't say, even when I found myself there, asking for Miss Levey, that I was very clear in my own mind as to why I had gone, but if anybody *had* been tampering with Evie, it was as likely to be the Jewess as anybody else.

She kept me waiting: a thing, I may say, that few people do nowadays. I waited in a matchboarded anteroom, among emancipated flappers and middle-aged disciples of Schmerveloff. Then Miss Levey herself came in as if by accident, and gushed out into apologies. She had had no idea it was I, she said; she did so beg my pardon.... She showed me into an inner room in which a hairy man, the single male-bird of the run, was expounding from a Blue Book to three or four more women; one of them was the lady who had participated in the intellectual courtship on the night of Aunt Angela's party. I turned to Miss Levey.

"I should like, if I may, to speak to you in private," I said.

She asked if Mr Boris's room was empty. The hairy man, looking up from his Blue Book for a moment, said that he thought so. She led the way into Mr Boris's room.

At the sight of her all my old dislike revived, and I found myself able to go straight to the point. I did so, without wasting a word.

"I've called to ask you, Miss Levey, whether you've given my wife the impression that I was the cause of your leaving the Freight and Ballast Company in order that room might be made for Miss Causton?"

She gave a shocked "Mis-ter Jeffries!" but I held up my hand.

"I know I'm putting it bluntly. You can be as blunt as you like also. Will you tell me whether that is so?"

"May I die, Mr Jeffries—but *surely* you know I'd arranged with Mr Schmerveloff long before!"

"I see. You dismissed us. Very well. Then let me put it in another form. Have you, in my wife's hearing, associated my name with Miss Causton's in any way whatever?"

The Debit Account

This time her answer was not quite so ready. When it came, it was a question.

"Do you mean lately, Mr Jeffries?"

"At any time, but especially lately."

Then she broke into glib speech, and all her "w's" became "v's."

"There, now I *knew* there vould be mischief before it was all over! 'Vot *is* the good of going into it?' I said; 'vot *is* the good, ven nobody even believed it at the time? Evie was there,'I said, 'and knew it was not true, so vy rake it all up now, Kitty?' I said. 'Ve all knew all about poor Louie,' I said, 'and vot's done's done anyway, and Evie doesn't vant to hear about it.'"

Here, suddenly tingling curiously all over, I interrupted Miss Levey. I spoke with a steadiness that astonished myself.

"One moment. You seem to be speaking of a definite occasion. Was this lately?"

Miss Levey was all pouting bosom, thick lips and fluent hands.

"Vy, *yes*! Ven Evie came here. Evie and Kitty and me, though vy I have Kitty here at all I don't know, seeing she makes slips in her work, and Mr Schmerveloff grumbles, and the other girls has it all to do over again——"

And the torrent continued.

I don't know what else she said; the rest didn't matter. Why it didn't matter you will see when I tell you that the tongue of a dead young libertine once, years before, had made free with Louie Causton's name and my own, and that the abominable slander, which had lasted for some days, had turned on nothing less than the paternity of Louie's child. All at the Business College, including Evie, had known of it; they had known, too, of the public apology I had been prompt to exact; but that mattered nothing, nothing, nothing now. This wretched little Israelite, revelling in her "v's," and even touching my sleeve from time to time, had seen to that. What the filthy rest was I do not know. Doubtless, beginning with that, and with the feeble Kitty to support her, she had made a complete history of jealousy.... And she did not even triumph openly. She lisped and protested, and put all on Kitty.... I left her, and almost fled from Louie also when, returning to Pall Mall, I encountered her coming out of Whitlock's room.

And now I have sat since lunch wondering what is to be done next. The afternoon hours have brought me no more light then those of the night did. Dully, I liken my life to that Maze at Hampton Court in which, one happy Sunday I don't know how long ago, Evie and I spent an hour. As then I seem to see Miss Levey's flamingo red behind the green hedges; she seems to lurk in my life, too wary to confront me, too malicious not to scratch. I am lost in winding intricacies. True, there is a door, even as there is a door at Hampton Court that is opened when the labyrinth is to be emptied. I find myself brought up against this door time after time, but I do not know what lies beyond it. You see what the door is: it is to tell Evie everything—everything.... Too wonderful Louie! Why, if you foresaw all this, did you not *make* me tell her—thrust me into a closet with her and keep the door until it was done—instead of letting me grope in my blindness and slip ever further and further away from her?... Oh, I am tired, tired.

I am too tired even to be angry for my poor practised-upon darling. For they have sprung this horrible thing upon her. Half the time she does not, cannot, believe it; of the other half of her life they have made a torment. Poor lamb! Of course if they are cruel enough they can make it seem plausible to her; I only wonder that, harrowed as she must have been for all these weeks, she has borne up at all. *I* know the horror she must have wrestled with!... That *that* wicked old story should crop up again!... But I must stop. Perhaps an hour's sleep will do me good.

The Debit Account

5.30 P.M.—That was a reckless thing to do, to go to sleep with these papers spread out on the table and my door unlocked. Not that my household is a staff of commercial collegiates, able to read this out-of-date old shorthand; but it was foolish for all that. Anyhow I am rather better, and think I can face the dinner to-night. After that I don't know what I shall do. I have not seen Evie all day.

I never felt less up to a dinner. But a little champagne will keep me going. They will be here in two hours and a half. It will take Evie an hour and a half to dress; I wonder what she is doing for the final hour! Dear heart, if she only knew how I ache to go up to her; but I must not do that until I have made up my mind what course to take. I shall have come to a resolution before I sleep to-night that will settle things one way or the other. We cannot stop at this *impasse*. I don't think Evie's is a real jealousy. To-morrow she will be sobbing on my shoulder that she has harboured it. But at present it has the venomous effect of the real thing, and if I do not put an end to it, it will recur. Let me think....

Again it comes upon me—why do I write this at all, that I shall most certainly be destroying? I have hardly the heart to think it out, but as it may have some bearing on what I shall have to say to Evie presently I must. I don't think it's that I'm urged to set myself right with anybody, even with myself. At first, when I began, I thought it was that—the need for self-justification—but now I don't think it's a question of justification or condemnation at all. It is a far more essential question. Suppose we call it the question of the personal standard....

I dare say my standards pass for low. That physical basis of marriage, for example, may pass for low—I'm sure it must to that ardent young couple who pant for intellectual companionship and Schmerveloff. And I confess that several of the Beatitudes are beyond me. To tell the truth I am not really at home with anything much higher than the best of human intelligence; and when I hear people speaking glibly of "man-made laws," I recognise that some folk are on terms of affability with Omnipotence that are denied to me. I suppose I am temperamentally reluctant to alter as much as a regulation once it is established, and I am certainly not ready with divine amendments to everything of man's offhand. Man's law I hold to be a necessarily imperfect, but roughly sufficient measure of man's conduct, and in the light of that law I may presently have a murder to confess.

I say *a* murder, not murder. Is there a difference? I do not know, and I am too weary to split hairs about it. Call them, if you like, one and the same thing. Still, if the one command be absolute, for the other a case may be stated. Do I, then, write to state a case?

But state it to whom? There is one Addressee to whom I have not lifted up my eyes. I, proud and conquering whom among my fellow-worms, have found the lesser law press hard on me, but I have not straightway invoked the greater. Man's decrees I have found strong and wise and admirable; the other is too wonderful for me. And this is the conclusion I promised you. To man, man's law is of more consequence than God's. Perhaps the damned are not utterly damned, so long as they do not add presumptuousness to their error. To have appealed and to have had that appeal rejected *were* damnation.... I do not appeal.

Nor can I see that I state my case to man. Nay, for I confess man's authority, lest it should appear that I do not, I shall destroy these papers. To-night or to-morrow I shall destroy them. Man shall not say that I have shirked the human issue. I refuse to plead at all. Let any who take it upon themselves to accuse or defend me plead or charge what they will. I am mute. I burn this....

I am tired....

And yet one boon I do crave. Perhaps those standards of mine, by their very lowness, may be the evidence, not of a smaller, but of a larger conception of Him Who Reigneth than might at first glance appear....

I am tired....

But all this advances me little with my resolution. Indeed, a fresh glare has just broken in on my brain. I was looking back a few moments ago on that long chain of circumstances with which my darling has been torturing herself—that old slander, innocencies between Louie and myself possible to have been misconstrued, my coming upon her that night in Billy's top room, Evie's own temperamental bias against Louie's profession, her silences, her belief of the calumny. Had Miriam Levey but known of my visit to the Models' Club and that strange walk of ours on the night of the Berkeley dinner, her case had indeed been complete! I had been reviewing all this, I say; and suddenly it struck me, suppose I do tell her? *What then?*...

Do you see—as the terrible Louie had seen—what then? I am supposing that the revelation did not kill her; do you see what then?

At last I saw it, and groaned. What then? Why, what but that I had put another before herself? What but that, while she had shared my board and bed, that fatal burden of my honour and confidence and trust had gone to another? What but that Louie, after all, *had* had the key and password of my life that I had denied to herself? What could I answer did she live to say, "What, you married me without telling me this? You tell me *now*, after having concealed it until concealment is no longer possible? You give me, *now*, something she's had the use of and has passed on to me? What is she to you, then, that *I* am not? Where do I fall short as a wife that *I* couldn't have borne this for my husband or died trying to bear it? Take it. Give it to her. She can have it. Fool, that I couldn't see this for myself, but must have Miriam Levey to point it out to me!"

Oh, my dear, my dear, my dear! We had never a fair start....

I do not know whether she intends to spend the night in the nursery again....

Seven o'clock. I must dress. And I must drink something now, or I shall never get through the evening....

And even yet I have not come to my decision.

11.30 P.M. This page at least it will be almost superfluous to destroy. My hand shakes like dodder-grass. That is the liquor I have drunk, but I had to do it.

They have gone. As I thought would be the case, I have had to play Evie's part too. That's twice Billy Izzard has seen me do that, for to-night was to all intents and purposes a repetition of that other night, when I tried to silence the voice of a gramophone by jumping up and bawling out an overstrained merriment. I don't mean that I jumped up and bawled to-night, of course. I merely had a number of flowers removed from the table, so that my eyes had a straight lane to Evie's at the other end, and sent down smiles and encouragement and support to her. And I allowed the men a bare ten minutes afterwards before I hurried off to her aid again. That and plenty of champagne; and I think I pulled it off. Billy, who lingered behind until I turned him out, says everything went splendidly. He didn't know I'd such gaiety in me, he said.

And Evie has gone to the nursery, but is not going to stay there. She told me that, with a hot little kiss, and a grip of her moist hand.... This was on the stairs, and she whispered (*words illegible*), and she had to run away so that the gratitude in her eyes would not run quite over—but that she whispered (*words illegible*)....

I shall do it to-night, unless my tongue is as shaky as my hand. There is a perfect stillness in my brain. I can see the whole thing spread out in my mind like a map; never

The Debit Account

have I been so triumphantly the master of a thing ... (*words illegible*).... The map is as steady as a rock, too; I turn my attention from it for a moment, choosing the form in which I shall present this aspect of the case or that, and when I return to the map it hasn't moved. Words, whole phrases, rise up in my mind, all so perfect that there will hardly be any shock at all. Evie cannot help but see it as I see it, and then I shall beg her pardon that I didn't tell her long ago. I have never loved her as I love her to-night, and those lovely pools of her eyes on the stairs (*words illegible*).

At last we are going to have a fair start. We hadn't that, you know. I still think I was right to stand between her and much of life, but this other thing was really too huge to be hidden. And she will not be jealous any more of Louie when I tell her that though Louie dragged all this out of me—she's no idea really how clever Louie is—my pulse has never quickened at Louie's touch nor my eyes brightened when they have met hers. "With my body" I have worshipped Evie, and shall (*words illegible*).... And so to-morrow will be a new beginning for us. I am rich; I have power; my only desire is now almost within my grasp. It was nonsense I wrote an hour or two ago—or perhaps it was the other day—about this only being the beginning of a deathless jealousy between those two. Evie will see. I shall make it all perfectly plain. I could almost do impossibilities to-night, with the words running like quicksilver in my mind and that chart I have in my brain steady as a rock. And if the anticipation of peace is such bliss, what will the peace itself be?...

I suppose she will be ready about twelve. I mustn't let this wondrous stillness of my brain slip from me. I was clever enough to foresee that it might, and so had the tray of liqueurs sent down here. But it doesn't do for an abstemious man to mix his liqueurs; the brandy again, I think. (*Several lines undecipherable*). I have only been drunk once in my life; I forget when that was; and once I shammed drunk; I don't suppose I shall ever be drunk again. A moment ago I felt a twinge where I made that dent in my head on the corner of Aunt Angela's fender, but it has passed.... It was a good dinner-party; I saw to that.... Evie, sweetheart—she'll be ready about twelve....

It is a quarter to now. I must be getting up. But first I must put these papers away. One of them slipped away somewhere a few minutes ago; I stumbled and upset a pile of them, but gathered them all up again, all but that one; never mind, I will look for it in the morning. It was my foot that slipped, not my brain. My brain is all right....

Well, it will be all right to-morrow....

END OF JEFFRIES' JOURNAL

ENVOI SIR JULIUS PEPPER DICTATES

The Debit Account

ENVOI

"Er—Miss Causton—can you stay for an hour or so? No, a private affair; I hope it's not inconvenient; thanks, and if I might give you supper afterwards?...

"Fact is, it's about poor old Jeffries. Better date it, and keep it safe. They've asked me to write something about him, and I'm no writer; but Izzard's found me a man who'll lick it into shape if I supply the material. 'Just talk it anyhow,' he said. Easily enough said, about a chap like Jeffries....

"You've seen this cutting, of course? No, not the first one; this from this morning's paper, about Mrs Jeffries. By Jove! it has followed quickly; awful! (By the way, you once met her, didn't you?) No, I want this copy; you can get another to-morrow; I'll read it out:

TRAGIC DEATH OF A LADY

We have to report a melancholy sequel to the death of Mr James Herbert Jeffries, of the Exploration and Mercantile Consolidation, Pall Mall, which was announced in our issue of the 10th ult. The circumstances of Mr Jeffries' sudden demise are still fresh in the public mind. The deceased gentleman, it will be remembered, succumbed to an attack of cerebral hæmorrhage brought on by strain and overwork and culminating on the night of a dinner-party given by him at his mansion in Iddesleigh Gate. It is with the deepest regret that we now announce that his widow has survived him only a few weeks.

We understand that during the intervening time the bereaved lady had occupied herself by going through the private papers of her late husband, sitting up late at night in order to render this last devout service. At about three o'clock yesterday morning Ann Madeley, a housemaid in Mrs Jeffries' employ, suffering from insomnia, had recourse to a medicine closet, situated where the servants' quarters adjoin the dwelling parts of the house. Her attention was attracted to a strong smell of escaping gas. She woke James Baines, a butler, and the two, wisely refraining from striking a light, made their way in the direction from which the smell of gas seemed to come. This brought them to their mistress' room. Obtaining no answer to their knocks, an entrance was forced, and in a small dressing-room lately used by Mr Jeffries——

"I hope this doesn't distress you too much, Miss Causton——

—Mrs Jeffries was found, fully dressed, stretched on a couch. The doors and windows had been closed, and a gas-fire turned on. We understand from Baines that Mrs Jeffries had remained as usual downstairs in the library until a late hour; and a page of notes in her husband's shorthand which has been found under one of the pillars of the writing-table——

"I've got that page of notes, by the way.——

—is sufficiently eloquent testimony as to what her sad duty had been. Dr McKechnie, who was at once summoned, certified that life had been extinct for some hours. The deceased lady, who was a great favourite in society, leaves two children in the care of a maiden aunt, Miss Angela Soames. The inquest is fixed for Tuesday next.

"Sad business, sad business.... Afraid they'll have to bring it in suicide—through grief, probably....

"Well, let's put it down as it comes. Of course he was a big man; lived an intense crowded life too. I should say at a guess there weren't many things he hadn't done at one time and another, short of committing a murder or a matrimonial infidelity. Don't think he could have been tempted to do that. One woman could do anything she liked with him, but the others wouldn't have much chance. Oh yes, a full life. Did you know, Miss

Causton, that the man who first passed him over to me found him helping to pick a fallen horse up in Fleet Street, when he hadn't a penny to his name? He was a commissionaire once.... As you know, he was the steam of this concern; it was the chance of my lifetime finding him, poor chap. Extraordinary man! He used to go at things by a sort of intuition; he tried to explain it to me, but I never could understand it. Once I said something about 'scientific method'; but he said it wasn't scientific method at all. Scientific method, he said, was something purely empirical, concerned with investigation, and not practically constructive in the least. Constructiveness came after. His method, he said, was based on the truths of art, 'the only truths we know anything about,' he said, whatever he meant. I never could follow him at all.... Well, if that's so, it rather explains a lot of these business giants going in for collecting—I mean it isn't that they just have the money to gratify their artistic tastes. But, as I say, I could never make head nor tail of it.... Which reminds me; that paper that got wafted under his desk; that was a dabbling in art in its way; fiction; did you know he tried his hand at fiction, Miss Causton? Here it is—an odd page—Whitlock knows a bit of shorthand, and he transcribed it for me:

'—*show him that red thing on the floor, and that curved thing on the door.*'

But now Archie in his turn seemed to have become divided. He had suddenly turned white. But an habitual pertness still persisted in his tongue. I don't think this had any relation whatever to the physical peril he seemed at last to have realised he was in. I stood over him huge and black as Fate.... 'Spare him if you can,' *that generous bloodthirsty devil in me muttered quickly....*

'Merridew,' *I said heavily,* 'you'll disappear to-morrow morning—or——'

'Shall I?' *he bragged falteringly....*

"And so on——

His only chance now was to have screamed aloud; but he did not scream. Instead he stooped quickly, caught up the poker, and struck at my head with it.

"And that's the end of the page. Sort of grim tale he would write. Queer hobby for a mercantile and political giant, wasn't it? But I'd go in for fiction myself if I thought it would make me like him.

"Verandah Cottage—that was no place for a chap like him. I hated to see him there. He could always go anywhere, meet anybody, was on equal terms with the best—and he without antecedents that I ever heard of, standing out solitary against a black background, just genius.... I wonder who his people were! Something uncommon, or else he was just a gigantic 'sport'——

"Of course—*de mortuis* and so on—but he did marry the wrong woman. To tell the truth, she was as ordinary as they make 'em; would have looked her best in the lights of the Holborn Restaurant at half-past six, waiting with the rest of the shop-girls for her bus home. He was a mass of contradictions, and one of 'em was that he merely idealised her. Pretty, of course, but poor Jeffries could have done better for himself than that. She never could bear me.... Well, there's nothing to be said now, poor creatures.... But sometimes it made me almost angry that he hadn't married the woman he ought....

"Well, let's begin with the day he first came to the F.B.C.——"

And Louie's pencil flew on.